The Seventh Day

By Ian Shurville

"And this gospel of the kingdom shall be preached in all the world for a witness unto all nations; and then shall the end come."

Matthew 24:14

Acknowledgements

As with any big undertaking there are usually lots of people who help you get through it. It is no different in my case. Simple acknowledgements to those people who have helped me create this story aren't enough. What comes to mind is gratitude. My appreciation and gratitude by words alone will fall short, but it is the only medium I have to say thank you. First, I would like to thank Debra Smith my editor, if not for her expertise, guidance and teachings none of what you are about to read would have ever made it to the page. I could have never done this without you. Secondly, to Samantha Hogg, who assisted me with making sure all my commas and quotations marks were in the right place and acted as my second set of eyes. She also managed my webpage, Facebook and Twitter accounts. Thank you, Sam.

Finally to my wife, Cindy, who for years encouraged me to write this book. Her belief in me was always there when I didn't think I could do it. Thank you, Honey.

Dedication

This book is dedicated to my children, Melanie, Jennifer, Christopher and Sarah who have always been and continue to be the best part of my life. Also to Audrey, my first grandchild, first of what I hope will be many more.

I love you all.

.

Prologue

65 Million Years B.C.

Three nervous raptors ran through the thick green foliage, twitching and blinking in silent communication. The air was pungent with the scent of rain soaked peat and drops clung desperately to the feathery leaves before falling into the pools below. It had rained for almost a week on and off. Reservoirs in the layers of decaying fauna teemed with insects that were busily digesting the ragged leaves, creating the perfect groundwork for the continuation of life.

The raptors, with their perfectly tailored snakelike skin, had bodies of pure muscle that melded form and function. Today's function: food. Moving in packs through the damp forest, they ran with snouts slightly raised and ears tuned expectantly. Like bandits skulking through the night, they moved in the direction of the watering hole. As they drew closer and closer to the target, the three increased their communication, speeding up their eye and head movements, using their inborn gift of cooperation.

Head down, sucking up water through her arched neck, a brachiosaurus sensed a movement slightly beyond her line of vision. Her massive size dwarfed the surrounding trees. Apprehensive, she lifted her head, water dripping from her snout. The newly created waterhole had been a welcome find in her yearly migration. Her two babies stayed close, watching their mother for warning signs. Others of her kind were crowded around the waterhole, enjoying a break from their trek. Alerted by the movement, they raised their heads and nervously scanned for the coming danger.

The raptors skulked through the bushes like a SWAT team. Quickly choosing a victim, they eyed their target and moved in, making a slight squishing sound as their claws sunk softly into the peat-laden ground. The tropical forest reached almost to the edge of the waterhole. They had eight feet of cover until they were at the shore. The screech of a pterodactyl could be heard above, its outstretched wings creating a change in air pressure that the raptors could sense. They inched closer, saliva dripping from their jaws, teeth moist in preparation for the kill.

One baby brachiosaurus wandered closer to its mother, as if it was aware of the danger. She turned her head to glance at him and confirm his presence.

The raptors took their position. One settled on the left side, momentarily looking back at the others. The second raptor moved slightly off center to the prey, the third took the right flank, waiting to attack. Glancing around one last time, the center raptor moved in and their victim sensed the closing of the gap.

At that moment came a sudden screech, and a flurry of branches and the other dinosaurs scattered. In surprise and desperation, the mother let out a hollow bellowing sound, beckoning her babies. She turned her head around to see what had happened. Just behind her was a Tyrannosaurus Rex with blood dripping from its teeth, a crushed and mangled raptor struggling in its jaws. The huge dinosaur stood in triumph with its meal for the day before pivoting off into the forest. Carrying its kill, the T-Rex moved quickly, its massive legs pounding the ground, leaving broken tree branches dangling in its wake.

The brachiosaurus gathered her babies and moved on, relieved to be alive.

The T-Rex felt the raptor's blood drip down its

throat as it moved through the tropical forest. The taste of blood was tantalizing and it waited impatiently to devour its catch. With lizard-like movements it jerked its gigantic head from side to side searching for landmarks. Under its long strides, anything living was instantly crushed and the indented landscape was changed forever.

When its final destination appeared, the T-Rex dropped its prey. Pale and hungry, her offspring caught the scent of the dead raptor that the T-Rex nudged towards it. After another push, her baby's poor vision finally fastened on the kill. Its tiny eyes focused on the raptor. It jumped on the body quivering with excitement and began to rip the skin away from the already tooth marked carcass. The raptor's blood dripped away from its body forming small pools that slowly seeped into the ground. Insects instantly swarmed around the warm red spots.

Finally, the mother T-Rex moved in to enjoy some of her reward. With her giant jaws, she ripped off the head of the raptor and with one bite crushed and swallowed it whole, looking skyward to let gravity do its job. She watched as her baby ripped, tore and swallowed the remains. In no time the entire raptor had disappeared and only a few bones remained.

The mother T-Rex and her baby rested together after the meal, the baby snuggling up close as if in thanks for the food. They fell asleep.

The T-Rex awoke to the screech of a pterodactyl, a normal sound around her nest. But something else was wrong. The air that usually flowed effortlessly into her large lungs was not reaching them. Her breathing began to quicken. Gasping for air, she tried to move as the muscles began to twitch in her hind legs. Pain began to move around her body and she stretched over to nudge her baby. Pushing dirt aside with her snout, she blew air through her nose to wake it up. There was no movement. She tried again - nothing. Anxiously she attempted to move her large frame, moving her legs in position to support her immense weight but she collapsed under her own mass. She tried again and, frustrated, she roared in defiance, straining to awaken her sluggish muscles. Nothing.

She crawled closer to her little one. There was no response; her baby was dead.

Another bellowing roar echoed through the forest. Pushing and pulling her numb limbs, she struggled for closeness.

One hour later her breathing had stopped. She

had positioned herself with her baby in a final act of love. All around the area the scene was repeated. Large and small dinosaurs could be heard from afar, the sounds of their desperate calls for help ranging from hideous shrieks to bellows and screams of misery.

One month later the only sound was the gentle rustle of the wind in the trees. The rain continued to fall as mud formed around the dead, encasing them for others to find like a postcard from the past.

Chapter 1

April 2nd
Hell Creek Formation, Montana

Matthew Redmond headed north on Highway I15 on the way back to his dig. Inside his well-used, British green Jeep Cherokee, Metallica was pounding out of the speakers. He was feeling as washed out as the prairie grasslands and trying hard to stay awake after a night spent in Butte, meeting with the local paleontologist to provide a show and tell about his findings. Matt was not a big fan of these functions. The inferior questions and lots of local "wisdom" from the would-be experts wore him out. It was a necessary evil, repeated monthly to keep the county association in the loop about his work with a progress report. The mayor and various other government officials always tagged along so they could at least pretend to understand what was going on. He understood he had to do it. It was part of the job and a requirement of the council grant.

Matt looked older than he was. At 35 he was often mistaken for a man in his mid forties and he was used to being called "sir" by guys his own age. The lines that the wind and sun had engraved in his face made some people mistake him for a cowboy instead of the paleontologist that he was. He didn't correct them. Many days spent crouched low to the ground with the sandy wind blowing around had already sculpted the face that time had been planning to give him. Today he felt as old as he looked. He pulled the Jeep up in front of the dig, and headed for his trailer.

The beige and brown trailer had melded into the Montana hillside. Perched on top of a ravine, it overlooked the barren landscape that was his workplace. It had been sitting with its wheels sinking into the same sandy ground for eighteen months. It was an hour's drive to the nearest town, Jordan, population 365, in the county of Garfield and underneath it all ran the Hell Creek Formation, a paleontologist's dream.

Matt headed straight for his bed, a modified cot with lots of padding, and was asleep within ten minutes. A few hours later, he pushed his way out of a deep sleep as he heard someone calling his name.

"Morning Matt.," Gillian said as she made her way

through the door, valiantly trying to knock the sand off the bottoms of her steel-toed boots on the doorframe.

"Morning," he replied, barely looking up.

"How did it go last night?" asked Gillian.

"Well, let's just say it went. Part of the job, I guess."

Matt called Gillian his right hand woman. She knew that he was not being unsociable; Matt was just not a morning person.

In various trailers set down in the middle of nowhere, Matt and Gillian had worked together for the last two years, first six months at Hadean Corp, in the badlands of Alberta, Canada, the next eighteen months digging in the Montana dirt. Gillian wanted to work with the best. She had accomplished one of her goals.

Gillian's other goal was to dress comfortably at all times in faded, ripped blue jeans and an old t-shirt while she lived the life of a paleontologist. She had found the perfect way to combine her keen observational skills with her deep dislike of offices.

"So Matt, while you were gone yesterday, Gordon from GeneQwest Group showed up, asking all kinds of questions. Do you know the guy?"

"Nope. Gordon who? I don't know anyone by

that name."

"I have his card somewhere in the trailer. I'll put the coffee on and try to find it."

The trailer was a little tight inside. If it was neater, there would have been more room but neither Matt nor Gillian was willing to play housekeeper. It was a dual purpose office and bunkhouse all in one.

Gillian rummaged around looking for the card. One half of the Formica table, which was permanently attached to the floor, was piled up with empty pizza boxes, empty beer and water bottles and paper plates. The other half was covered in reference books, papers and a computer. Lifting old research papers and random American Paleontology magazines, she looked around anxiously.

"I know it's here, I put it right around here," she said, pointing to the end of the table that held all their paperwork, filed geologically, with the latest items on top.

"Hold on, just let me think. I came in, put my bag down, then…" She moved with confidence in the direction of the table. Out from under some papers on the corner, she yanked the card high in the air.

"See, I am organized, just need a little time to refresh my memory," she said, handing the card to him.

"Gordon Lynch, GeneQwest International Group, Chief Executive Officer," Matt said with a frown. Never heard or seen this guy before. Why the hell would the CEO be wandering around our dig?"

"Mainly he was interested in talking to you."

"So, did you get lots done while I was away?" asked Matt.

"Yes," she replied, "I got the bone density results back from Crescent Labs, all what we had predicted."

"Ok great," Matt said, his concentration already fixed on the day's work. "So today let's work on the major hind leg, I think there are some interesting things happening there."

"Ok, I'll meet you out there in 5 minutes."

"Give me ten," replied Matt.

Gillian swung out the door and jumped down to the Montana sand leaving her boot prints in the sandy gravel. Matt stretched to give his body a last chance for comfort before he got up. His feet touched the end of the black metal bunk. He pushed a little harder trying to increase the size of the bed as he did every morning. It never worked.

He groped around with his feet, trying to find the old plaid slippers he had placed near the bed the night before, knowing the floor would be either cold or sandy. Today it was the latter. He headed immediately to the coffee machine. It was empty; yesterday's grinds were still inside. He stuck his head out of the trailer looking for Gillian. She was already heading for the dig.

"Hey Gillian, I thought you said you were making coffee?" he said, empty coffee pot in hand.

"Right, sorry about that Matt. Two sugars and a bit of cream in mine," Gillian called back.

Scratching his head, then his butt, he headed for the toilet. His morning rituals never changed, even in the field. Soon the ten minutes were up.

Chapter 2

April 6th
The Dig

Matt headed downhill to the dig. The feel of the soft sand under his boots reassured him he was home and renewed his confidence. Matt knew from an early age that he would be working in dirt, and he pushed himself to graduate from MIT.

Today, because of his careful, calculated work that dirt was hopefully going to reveal what had happened at this place 65 million years ago. These dusty surroundings were a far cry from the tropical oceans and forests that had existed here before. For the last 18 months he'd been commissioned by Andros Corp., a subsidiary of GeneQwest, to uncover the secrets of that ancient time and Matt never shied away from a good challenge. It was something his father had instilled in him. For a moment, he wished his Dad were still alive to share in his success, then, with a sigh, he pushed the thought away.

The site was surrounded by border tape that made it look like an unlikely crime scene on the rugged landscape. Shovels of various sizes were wedged randomly in the sand while brushes, digging knives and dental picks lay close at hand on the edge of the pit. The larger rocks surrounding the site had already been moved to the side by heavy equipment that had been there months before.

Matt and Gillian had been supervising the site for what seemed too long without any results. When Gillian bounced out of the trailer anxious to start the work for the day, her enthusiasm often rubbed off on Matt. Today was one of those days. He thought he might need her optimism if they didn't find what they were hoping for.

The rest of their team consisted of four graduate students, all on summer break and keen to learn from Matt. He had a reputation that was almost legendary in some circles due to his other well-documented discoveries. His work in the Yixian formation in China had produced a finely feathered microraptor specimen. It clearly supported the theory linking modern day birds to dinosaurs and after it made the cover of National Geographic, there was no turning back to a quiet life.

The dig had progressed down to the layers that

counted. After the sedimentary topsoil had been peeled back, the exposed dirt began to warm to a sun it hadn't seen in millions of years. The sides of the dig were angled and supported to avoid a collapse. It was the worst thing that could happen after all their hard work and Matt had made sure the sandy-coloured records of time were properly held back.

Matt and Gillian were leading by example when their team showed up. The two of them were down on their hands and knees, scrapping, brushing, air blasting and doing what was needed to remove the dusty earth.

"So, can you see the shapes?" Matt asked Gillian.

"Yep. What do you think we're looking at?"

Matt did not answer right away. He wanted to be clear in his own mind first. He hesitated a little longer, thinking it over, and then replied with assurance. "That, my co-worker, is the hind tibia of a T-Rex, and it sure appears to be one large mother of a reptile," he said with a smile.

"So if you're right, this will be one for the books?" Gillian replied.

"I would say so. Now keep at it, so we can prove it."

Matt stood up and brushed the sand off his jeans.

Calling his crew over, Matt and Gillian climbed out of the pit and handed the dig over to younger eyes and knees.

The wind picked up and the smell of ozone floated through the air, signaling rain. The sky deepened to an ashen grey, while the clouds puffed up, getting ready to exhale. Matt looked over to Gillian, shrugging his shoulders. Rain was sometimes a good thing on digs, other times not. He watched for a minute to check the direction of the moving grey masses in the sky. They had been rained out three weeks ago in the middle of a summer heat wave. This area of Montana was known for its weird weather. It was mostly arid, but when it did rain, it was usually torrential.

"So are we close to where we need to be, if we want to finish before the bad weather sets in?" asked Gillian.

"I think so," Matt said, reaching for his coffee cup. "I think within the week we should be where we need to be. The schedule says we should be seventy five percent through in September and it's only August."

"What's the rush Matt? Do you have any idea why GeneQwest is in need of what we find out here?"

"Nope, Gill, I don't, but I know we are being paid good money to recover this specimen and we shall deliver," he said in a military tone.

"Yes captain!" Gillian replied, pretending to salute.

Matt decided not to take any chances. He shouted out for the team to head back to their temporary campsite and batten down the hatches in case of a downpour. There was thousands of dollars worth of equipment stored there from sonar monitors to analytical gyroscopes that needed protection.

Within minutes windows were shut, doors sealed and essentials had been taped, wrapped or tied down. Matt and Gillian headed back to the trailer to get ready for the rain.

As raindrops pelted the large, dirty white tarp covering the dig, the wind moved it back and forth like a bellows. The team was apprehensive. A little rain would just muddy the site but too much rain would make mudslides.

Matt sat in the trailer, logged on to the Internet, checking the weather conditions for the area. The weather report hadn't said anything about rain and it still showed the same faulty forecast.

The rain increased, coming down at a forty-five degree angle, slipping under the tarp. Small streams of water began to trickle down to the pegs that held the tarp in place. The water moved downhill toward the plains after it left the site, winding around like a snake. The weather began to get worse, more rain, more water and more runoff.

Suddenly the left peg came loose and the tarp fell into the pit, creating a lopsided cover. Water began pooling on top of the tarp. With a snap, the peg on the right side pulled free and the tarp folded back on itself, exposing the top half of the dig. The rain pelted down, forming streams full of dirty brown water that washed along pebbles and small plants that had lost their foothold.

"Matt!" shouted Gillian, "Are we hanging in till it finishes or heading back to town before the road back gets washed out?"

He stuck his head out of the trailer, making an assessment.

"Let's hang in there for just a little longer. I see the sky clearing about two miles away."

The students were huddled in their tent waiting for orders. They couldn't leave even if they wanted to. They glanced at each other or scanned the skies, wondering what would happen.

Suddenly, a flash of lightning lit up the prairie and thunder cracked like shattered glass. The rain picked up its tempo. At that moment Matt decided to head back to the site for a final check. He felt a tremor through the heel of his worn Red Wing boots and a shudder ran up to his hips.

He hurried to the edge of the dig, where he could see that the tarp had now disappeared down the slight slope and was being dragged away by the water. He couldn't believe what he was seeing. He was paralyzed, unable even to call Gillian over. He stood like a mannequin, drenched to the skin, staring with amazement. This was big - very big.

A smile broke over Matt's face as he stood on the bank looking down at the dig. He was getting wetter and wetter with each passing minute but he didn't care.

Slowly, like a curtain being raised on a monument, bones were surfacing as the water moved the sand away from his find. The wind made him shiver, but he didn't move.

After half an hour the rain began to let up. The flow of slurry stopped, leaving creases in the limestone and sand, like the lines on an old man's face. The occupant of the dig was now in plain sight.

Matt walked back to the trailer, his boots leaving imprints as he went. He opened the door of the trailer much too wide.

"Gillian!" he shouted.

"What the hell happened to you? Did you go for a swim and not tell me?" Gillian asked.

"I know, I know. I went out to make sure the tarp was secure, but I was too late. It had blown down the bank, but what I did see was amazing. It was an unveiling."

"What are you talking about?"

"You have to go out there and see for yourself. You won't believe it. I mean it's amazing. Quick, come on, let's go."

His excitement was hard to conceal and Gillian was a little surprised. Matt was usually pretty reserved.

"Ok, ok, I'll come. Let me get my rain slicker on."

"You won't believe what you're going to see."

Gillian put on her yellow raincoat, rubber boots and her matching yellow hat.

"Come on, come on," Matt said impatiently, waiting for her at the door.

"Ok, ok, I'm ready."

As they stepped down from the stairs of the trailer their feet sunk into the saturated soil and mud clung to their boots.

"Geez Matt, I have never seen you like this. It must be amazing."

"It is. It is. You'll be blown away," Matt said, leading the way.

They made it to the edge of the bank and stopped short where the ground was crumbling from the rain. Gillian and Matt stared into the dig without speaking. They couldn't believe their luck.

In front of them lay what they both knew was going to be one of the great fossil finds of the decade. It was every paleontologist's dream to find what they were looking at. Matt knew the importance of this, and he knew that Gillian knew it too.

"So dear, what do you think?" he asked.

It took a second for Gillian to answer.

"Well, I think you and I will be making lots of presentations around the world, that's what I think. Matt, this is incredible. You know what this means?"

"You're damn right I know what this means."

They gazed at the full fossil of a T-Rex with her offspring curled up right next to her.

"You see that corner over there?" Matt said, pointing to the left side of the dig.

"Yep, what about it?"

"You see the edge of the bone outline there, right where they're touching together?"

"Yep, I'm following you." Gillian moved her gaze around the area.

"Well, that, my associate, is a skin fragment, a fully attached tissue that has been left intact. It is not fossilized, so you know what that means?"

"Well, my esteemed colleague, I certainly do."

"Let's get down there and photograph every inch of this dig, and get that tissue into something that will preserve it, and let's do it quickly. You never know what can swoop down from the sky and pick it up for its next meal." Matt looked up, searching for the hawks that were always frequenting the dig. "You stay here and I'll go to the trailer and get the stuff."

"Ok hurry Matt, I'll keep guard," Gillian said, scanning the skies.

Matt ran back to the trailer, the mud on his boots making his feet heavier and heavier with each step.

He quickly looked around for a Petri dish and some propylene glycol to put the tissue in. Papers and magazines flew around the trailer as he pushed, kicked and shoved them aside, searching frantically for the collection material.

"Gillian," he shouted out, "where the hell is everything in this damn place?"

Chapter 3

Hands tucked into his pockets trying to stay warm, Gordon Lynch watched the procession. Another protest group with a cause was prancing down Lexington Avenue, spouting stupid words. He begrudgingly trailed a half block behind them until he spotted Grand Central.

His black, nicotine-smelling sport coat had its collar turned up to protect him from the wind, an open necked cream colored shirt stuffed with a burgundy cravat was no protection from the chill. Hoping to infuse some warmth back into his body, he ducked inside Grand Central Station and headed downstairs to a coffee shop.

Standing in line waiting for his turn to order he played with the lighter in his pocket. He wanted to have another cigarette; the last one had been stamped out on the sidewalk five minutes ago. He never could shake the habit.

An overstuffed manila envelope was threaded between his elbow and coat. Coffee in hand, warmer now, he weaved through the robotic commuters. As he pushed through the worn brass doors onto 42nd street, he felt the wind meet his face. He hunched down to lessen its impact and headed west towards the United Nations building. With two blocks to go, he wished he had remembered how cold the wind was off the Hudson River. He would have had the chauffeur drop him closer to his target.

At the corner of 1st Avenue and 42nd street, the constant honking of car horns and the distant chanting from the protestors blanketed the area with a layer of noise. The multi-colored country flags at the United Nations building were snapping stiffly at attention.

Crossing 1st Avenue, Gordon headed for the building next door. The warmth from Grand Central had worn off. He reached for the crushed red and white package of Winstons in his coat pocket, knocking out an unfiltered cigarette. Lighting up, he took a deep haul hoping it would warm him up again. Sheltering himself from the persistent breeze, he leaned against the corner of the building, cupping the glowing end of the cigarette in his hands trying to stay warm, all the while waiting for the first signs of his contact. A bystander might have thought he was looking for a fix.

The steady stream of black limos snaking around Manhattan was a common sight for New Yorkers. Chauffeured dignitaries, rock stars or politicians, New Yorkers paid no mind to any of them. They all represented the same thing - traffic jams, security check points, and an opinionated cacophony of honks, frustrated shouts and finger gestures.

Gordon stood watching the line of limos in front of the building as a religious leader stepped out of each car and into a cluster of photographers jostling for the perfect shot. Alerted by the news media, most Manhattanites knew the arrival of so many dignitaries would cause delays on the roads. It was all in the name of solving world hunger and third world poverty and they had heard it all before.

Gordon waited on the corner, still supporting the building, watching the final attendee exit his limo. A third Winston was lying extinguished on the cracked sidewalk. His phone pulsed against his pocketed hand and he quickly drew it out like a gunslinger ready to fire. A symbol on the screen indicated a new text had arrived. Scrolling through the icons, he opened the freshly minted text.

Coffee shop in the Hilton. 5 minutes.

Gordon had already passed the Hilton on his way over, this time the wind would be at his back. Columns of black tinted glass stretched skyward capped with white cloud puffs framing the Hilton sign. Constant winds coming off the Hudson tore through the display of flags that imitated the ones on the UN building.

Gordon approached the entrance that was guarded by two doormen dressed in long grey jackets trimmed in white. One doorman opened the door for him, nodding with a smile.

"Good Morning Sir, little cool this morning?"

"Thank you, yes, it is," Gordon replied.

Once inside, Gordon lowered his collar, looking around for the coffee shop.

He let the aroma of roasted beans lead him past the souvenir shop window with its rows of Lady Liberty statuettes lined up like soldiers ready for battle.

The familiar tightness in his chest began to build up. He was used to the sensation and readied himself for a bout of coughing. Two or three in a row were the usual. Preparing himself, he pulled a white embossed handkerchief out of his right coat pocket. After the fifth cough, he quickly glanced at the handkerchief, keeping watch for anything unusual. There was nothing. He deposited the handkerchief back into his pocket as he entered the coffee shop.

Tan colored booths along the window side were paired with the usual bistro styled circular tables. Gordon scanned the room searching for his contact. He spotted him in the last booth, checking his phone. Placing two one dollar bills on the counter, Gordon grabbed a ceramic mug with an orange insignia plastered on it, quickly poured a coffee and headed for the booth. Passing the various coffee makers and mugs for sale, he felt another coughing bout surfacing. Willing his body to suppress it, he slowed his stride until he felt it pass.

"Morning William," Gordon said, placing his mug down on the table.

William looked up from his phone and registered Gordon's frame in front of him.

"Morning Gordon, please sit down," he said, pushing his hand forward in anticipation of a handshake. Shaking hands, Gordon slid over on the opposite bench seat.

"First off, thanks for this impromptu meeting, I do appreciate it," said Gordon.

"No problem. I haven't seen you in years, so it was nice to hear from you."

"Same goes for me, William, I know it's been too long between visits. You know, life and business gets in the way and time just zips by."

"For sure," nodded William, "I can attest to that. So I know we talked briefly on the phone the other day and I told you I had about a one hour break from our UN meetings - not a lot of time - but you gave me the impression that you had something to ask of me, am I correct?"

"You are still that perceptive guy I remember from years ago. Yes, there is something I would like to ask of you."

William smiled back at him. "And what might that be, Gordon?"

"Well, I think it is an easy one," Gordon said, tongue in cheek.

"Ok, but I've seen your easy ones. Let's hear it."

"You know me too well. Why don't I just get it out of the way and we can spend the rest of the time reminiscing about old times?" said Gordon

"Sounds good to me, let me have it."

"William, I know you've moved up the ranks in

the Vatican. I have seen your star rising," joked Gordon.

William leaned back in the booth, his arms spread wide and almost reaching the ends of the seat. He motioned with one hand for him to get on with it.

Gordon knew the gesture. "So, here it is, I just need a package to get to the Pope. It's not a big package. I would like to get it to him quicker than the usual route. I know there is lots of security checks involved, but I was hoping you could move it along for me. It's nothing special, just a bunch of papers that I would like him to go over, something I think that will be beneficial to the Vatican and beyond. So my friend, can you help me?"

Moving forward in his seat, William looked directly into Gordon's eyes. "What the hell is in these papers that you think the Pope needs to read?"

"Well, let's just say, William, they could make a big difference to the organization. It's all good."

Raising his coffee mug, Gordon took a sip of the black liquid, waiting for an answer.

Grinning from one side of his mouth William replied, "So this won't affect my rising star will it?"

Gordon laughed, "No, it won't. Would I do that to you?"

"I'm not sure Gordon. I've watched your star

rising as well and at times it looks a little shaky," William said.

"Well, you know what it's like. The press gets hold of anything they think will sell papers. Yes, I have had a few, let's say "headlines," but never once have they proved anything, because they can't. I run on the right side of the law. I have to, otherwise I'd be shut down in an instant. You know what I'm saying, right?"

"I do," replied William, "I do. So is that the package you're talking about?" he said, pointing at the stuffed envelope sitting next to Gordon.

"Yep, that's it. Not too heavy for you is it?" Gordon said, lifting it off the seat and handing it to William.

"No, I think I can handle it. You know I have to go through the normal channels to get it to his Holiness. I figure that we should box it up for security reasons and just for more protection. This envelope won't make it very far without tearing apart."

"Ok, I have no problems with that. Do you want me to take it back and get it all prettied up for you?" smiled Gordon.

"No," said William, "Leave it with me. Should I open this and give it a read before I give it to the Pope?"

"That's up to you. You may just want to be on the sidelines for this one. I'm not sure where it's going to lead but I'm sure that you'll see things happen once the Pope reads the document."

Looking down at his phone, William saw a message pop up on the screen.

"Ok Gordon, I'll help you out on this one, but remember, I will be back in New York next month and you'll owe me. Not sure what that is at the moment, but I'll figure something out, and it won't be at a coffee shop." William smiled. "Now I have to get to a meeting," he said, picking up his phone and showing Gordon the message on the screen.

"No problem William, thanks again for your help. Believe me, next month when you're back in town, we can spend more time reminiscing and I'll foot the bill for a nice dinner. Wasn't Italian food your favorite?" asked Gordon.

"For someone your age, you have a good memory," laughed William.

"That's all I have left," replied a smiling Gordon.

"Sure it is. I'll look forward to the meal," replied William, heading for the exit. He turned back. "Gordon, before I go, is this opportunity - or whatever it is - going to another group, just to have another option? If you understand my meaning."

Smiling, Gordon offered William a cigarette. "You don't miss a trick do you William? We all have our gods, mine just happen to be green."

Gordon followed his lead and the pair exited the Hilton. Shaking hands one more time, they said their goodbyes.

"Oh William, I almost forgot, while you're handling this for me, do you think you could get me the telephone number of Bernard Manning? He's the Pope's secretary. He was a friend of my father's a long time ago. I just want to say hello. He must be getting up there in years."

"I will see what I can do, no promises on that one," William said, signaling goodbye again.

"Thanks William. I know you'll try your best."

The wind hit Gordon's lungs, pushing up a repressed cough. His muscles prepared for the convulsion as, handkerchief in hand, he headed uptown to his office.

Chapter 4

"Are you fucking kidding me Bernard? You can't be serious, after all the shit we're going through, all the shit we're fighting for, you're leaving to - where did you say?"

"I am leaving to go to Perugia."

"Perug-ga what? Where the hell is that?"

"Italy, you stupid Irishman, Italy. You know, Michelangelo, the Renaissance, all the famous artists and that woman you love...Sophia Loren?"

"There? Why the hell are you going there, why don't you just stay here?"

"Religious studies."

"Oh yeah, religious studies, sure. I bet it is. I know you Bernard, you love the women."

Bernard Manning and Padriag Lynch had been coming to The Swan ever since the two of them could pass for legal drinkers. It was their bar, their home, where they swirled their beers against the soft sheen of a polished leather counter which, after two centuries of holding up the drinks and elbows of well watered patrons, was starting to show its age. At the far end of the pub two men were aiming their darts at the board. The smell of stale beer and cigarette smoke enveloped the two best friends like a familiar embrace holding them to the bar. Twice a week they met to discuss what was wrong with their jobs and their lives and how they would change Ireland if they were in charge.

Bernard had been born in a town just west of Belfast and Padriag only left Belfast to take the family on their yearly vacation to Magilligan, an hour's drive away, always to the same holiday home at the seaside. The kids enjoyed it, even though it was usually cloudy and cool.

"Padriag, come on, you know we can't keep doing this to ourselves. This fighting and killing and hatred, it has to stop. I have had the calling. You know, the calling from the Lord," said Bernard, drink in hand.

"Bernard, I know you and I have talked about it for years, but I didn't think you were ever going through with it. And Italy, come on, that's a long fucking way from home. Jesus boy, you and I have lived here forever; you can't be serious about this shite are you?"

"Yes Paddy, I am. It's time for me to leave this place. I have decided to devote my life to the Lord, and I have to try to make a difference. I know it's the right time and the right thing to do."

"Come on, let's have one more pint. Maybe if you have a few more you might be changing your mind?"

"I will say yes to the pint, but I'm not changing my mind. I've thought long and hard on this one Paddy. It's time, it's time for me."

"Come on then, let's have a toast to your future and a toast to Ireland."

They raised their glasses with a muffled clunk and settled in to talk away the remaining hours of the night until the barkeep sounded the bell for last call. Paddy and Bernard left the pub together for the last time. Swaying slightly, they stood on the corner and gently punched each other on the shoulder.

"You'll be back." Padriag said, his voice thick and cracking as water rose behind his eyes.

"We'll see," Bernard replied, giving his friend a last shake to his shoulder. They turned and parted without a backward glance as they had always done.

The next morning at Padraig's was a typical

Saturday. The aroma of bacon, black pudding and eggs wafted through the small house. Gordon, 20 years old, handsome and hung over, came down the stairs, avoiding the creaking spots; he was the last one at the table.

"Morning, my son," said his father.

"Morning Father, how are you feeling today?" Gordon replied tongue in cheek.

"As good as you my boy, as good as you," said Paddy. "Your mother has made her world famous Irish breakfast. Come on, dig in before it gets cold."

"Yes Gordon, get right in there before your father finishes it all off," said his mother in her beautifully soft Irish accent.

"Ok, ok I will."

Gordon was finding it harder and harder to maintain the Saturday breakfast tradition as well as his new found tradition of late Friday pub nights.

"Guess what Bernard told me last night at the pub?" asked Padriag.

"I don't know Father, what?" Gordon replied sullenly.

"Tell us Padriag," said his mother, giving Gordon a sharp look.

"Well, he is leaving us. The bugger is leaving to

go to some place in Italy, and some place I can't even pronounce. I tried to talk him out of it, but it went nowhere, that son-of-a-bitch is determined."

"Paddy, watch your language," said his wife.

"Oh come on woman, they aren't little children anymore. They've heard worse. Haven't you all?"

Both Gordon and his sister nodded.

"See, Ruth, I told you. You are too protective of these two, let them grow up."

"Go on Padriag, finish the story about Bernard."

"I think we should all say our goodbyes before he disappears. I can't believe that my school buddy is leaving our Ireland. I think he is a bit of a traitor. He says that all this fighting has to stop, we can't keep doing this to ourselves and he wants to make a difference. I don't know what difference he thinks he is going to make in Italy, but good luck to him. He'll be back." Padraig stopped, blinked his eyes rapidly and pretended to focus on a bit of toast.

"I will miss him; I'll miss the little bastard," he said in a whisper. He got up from the table with his cup of tea in his hands and went to sit in his favorite chair.

"Gordon, let me tell you something," he said, raising his voice a little. "All this shite about religion and

God doesn't pay the bills. The bunch of us looking up to the sky for answers. The only answer I ever got was seeing me Mum die from some type of cancer and they didn't even know it was cancer back then. When we went to church to say our goodbyes, we were told that she had gone to a better place. Better place my arse; she left us to fend for ourselves. It was bloody hard, and the only advice I got from the Father at the time was to keep praying and God will answer your prayers. Well me boy, they were never answered. All I know was that I had to be at work the next day. That, son, is the reality of life. Never forget that. Answers don't come from the sky. You make your own answers to your own questions. He'll be back, mark my words. He'll be back."

Gordon listened to his father's attitude towards the church coming through in no uncertain terms. He realized then that faith, however prevalent it was throughout his life, had not produced the desired results for his father. He decided then and there that if he wanted results he would take matters into his own hands. Work for his father had become his faith, his measurement of success and living with the reality of everyday life had produced a man who was bitter and resigned.

The conversation resonated in Gordon's thoughts for years. Actions will always produce results, looking skyward would not.

Chapter 5

James Mitchell had driven the same route to work for the last three years. His three-geared bike served him well and he had never felt the need for more sophisticated transportation. It was the last vestige of his student life that remained since he left home and the halls of Cambridge.

He had intentionally taken the offer from Illumina Labs in Bristol as a chance to move out and move on. Living with his parents while attending university had given him the chance to help with the family finances but being the last one at home had not always been a good thing for James and he knew it.

His mother doted on him, preparing his lunches, doing his ironing and generally making sure that he was looked after. He was the star of the family in her eyes. It had somewhat strained his relationships with his two older sisters, but they kept in touch.

His father was a principal in an engineering firm who believed that there was a solution to every problem and James took this to heart and applied it to every aspect of his studies and his life.

He pulled up at the red light, pushing backwards on the pedals of his bike and waited for the light to go green. A light mist off the ocean settled over his slicker and hood and his glasses started to fog up. When the light changed, he started down the designated bike lane, squinting through his blurry lenses.

After a half hour bike ride he arrived at a heritage building situated between Wine and Castle Street. It sat in a redeveloped area that the city had successfully supported in hopes of revitalizing the retail trade. Illumina Labs had been there before the developers, and had converted an old warehouse to fit its needs. Warm wartime brickwork mixed with aluminum panels created a modern but nondescript facade. One black door held a brass plate with *Illumina Labs* etched on it. A doorbell on the right hand side was the only way to signal that someone was outside. Security was always important, and the request for a digital key had been put in months ago but nothing had been done yet.

James inserted a metal key into the lock and turned it to the right. He heard the deadbolt slip, turned the doorknob and stepped inside. He was the first one there this morning. He switched all the lights on with a sweep to the right and the bulbs struggled to light as if they needed waking up. Still wearing his knapsack, James pushed his bike through the warehouse and leaned it against the wall. The water dripping on the concrete floor would be dry soon enough.

As an honours graduate from Cambridge, he had fielded offers from various UK companies working on the latest developments in molecular genetics. Each one offered a lucrative and prestigious position to a young man fresh out of university. At 28, the outstanding leadership skills he had learned from his father complemented his graduate work. His ground-breaking work in DNA repair and RNA splicing made him a rising star. His applications of developmental genetics in simple organisms and its application to human genetics caught the old school off guard.

Illumina Labs had offered James a position as lead geneticist in what was essentially a startup. They recognized his brilliance and he saw an opportunity to work in his area of interest – the leading edge of the latest research. They had paid handsomely and he signed on for five years, with bonuses for targets that would make him a rich man.

James headed to his office located on the far side of the building, facing west. The pale sunlight peeked through the etched windows just long enough to reveal a thin layer of dust coating the bookshelves that lined the room. The old metal desk that anchored the room was a relic in comparison to what he could have ordered. Offered his choice of office furniture, he was happy with the desk that the carpenters had left behind after the renovation. It suited his modest nature. He was still somewhat embarrassed by all the accolades showered on him during his years at university; he just wanted to do good work, rigorous work, work that he could be proud of. He wasn't exactly pleased that his last professor had written a letter to *The Times* predicting his great impact on the world of genetics. His one concession to office decor was two new red chairs that sat in front of the desk. They simply appeared there one morning. James never even noticed them until a colleague came in and sat down in one of them. He liked his office to be organized, efficient and neat. Decoration was irrelevant. He modeled his work ethic after his father and took inspiration from a famous quote that was framed and hanging on the wall in his office: "God is in the details."

He knew where everything was and why it was there. His daily paperwork was put away into the adjacent locked file cabinet. Digital information was stored on his laptop and backed up by the mainframe. Every evening before leaving he made sure his desk was clear. His three computers and the mainframe server in New York churned numbers all through the night.

From his office he could see all the workspaces that made up the lab. Overhead lighting that hung from wooden trusses left behind from the warehouse conversion provided a warm glow to the open space. Tables were scattered with various sizes of beakers, containers and an assortment of recipes in Petri dishes and jars. Metal tweezers, test tube clamps and brushes were scattered on the stainless steel counter top. Divided up into quadrants, each section was dedicated to various teams and tasks were assigned by James. Every team had a lead researcher coordinating activities, who funneled results back to him.

Illumina had attracted the best scientists they could afford to assist him with his research. Nate from South Africa specialized in molecular anatomic pathology,

Kate from Detroit lead efforts in immunology, Peter, the local content from Bristol coordinated research in malignant disorders and finally Sara from New York concentrated on genome therapy. Together with James, the four formed the backbone of Illumina, GeneQwest's genetic research arm.

James was dubious about Sara's appointment to the team. She was connected to a board member at GeneQwest, so it appeared that she was chosen as a favour to someone rather than as a result of a search for the best and brightest. All the other team members were selected based on proven aptitude in their respective fields. Sara's capabilities, insight and contributions soon proved James's initial reservations wrong. At 33, her enthusiasm for the work combined with a feminine touch offered a different perspective to the analytical side of the research. She was the only team member to display a sign in her office that read, "Our Lab, a Place of Discovery and Enlightenment." James admired her spirit.

Comparative genomics was Illumina's line of business. It was an emerging science that was at the forefront of genetic research, right where James wanted to be. Their mandate from GeneQwest was clear, analyze the DNA sequence patterns of humans against other organisms to find the similarities that had stood the test of time, the differences that had caused new species to emerge, and, most tantalizing to James, the elements whose nature was still undefined.

The similarities between humans and various animals were startling. Research had already established that gorilla DNA was closest to humans, followed by chimps. Even mice had a ninety-eight percent match to human DNA. But within that one percent was the magic formula formed by the nucleotides that made up the structure of the RNA based on their position in the gene sequence. The single strands of RNA directed the synthesis of proteins and were the building blocks of many viruses. That formula grew fur or feathers, made tails appear or disappear and created the human mind that would eventually make sense of it all.

The worldwide Genome project had been just the beginning. Now the race was on to capitalize on the research, patent new gene technology and bring it to market. GeneQwest's unlimited budget was harnessed to identify the proteins within chromosomes that caused them to change their usual normal arrangement into one that created disease. One altered protein could cause cancer, heart and kidney disease – or cure it.

James knew that GeneQwest would benefit from any of these cures; he knew how the game would be played. His personal mandate was to discover the cure for anything that would help mankind. He included that in his acceptance letter, knowing full well that their eyes were only on the bottom line. Their aim was to be the most profitable player in the game, with the most patents, and the most research results.

That was three years ago, and they had nearly achieved their goal. The CEO made sure of that.

At fifty-two, Gordon Lynch was the face of GeneQwest, his sizeable genetics company ran in tandem with his many smaller subsidiaries, Illumina being one of them. His street smarts mixed with business savvy, made him popular with the board members. His hard-nosed business reputation was admired by the shareholders and praised by the investment community.

Gordon enjoyed the finer things in life and his assortment of Rolex watches and Armani suits flashed the right image to the outside world. He used the web and personal interviews to elevate his profile and his empire. Shares always increased after his appearances. His tagline of "Always demand results" was something the shareholders loved to hear and he loved to provide them with it.

He lived in Scarsdale, New York, with his wife Jessica and put down roots in the upscale neighborhood. Their two children, Ben and Kendra, grew up in the well-heeled community, connecting with the children of other prominent businessmen.

The rebirth of Bristol was a microcosm of England reinventing itself, a unique blend of British values merging with new commerce. The city provided homes for Hewlett Packard and a multitude of up and coming tech firms. It boasted about its universities and three theological colleges. Illumina had arrived with little fanfare. The announcement in the local paper of yet another American firm was of little interest to the predominately blue-collar workforce. A total of ten people would be employed at Illumina, nothing a union was interested in.

Gordon liked being close to Ireland, even though the memories of his father's involvement in the Protestant movement that led to his family's eventual move to New York had hurt him at the time. He remembered the long discussions his father had with friends, the heated words that always ended up with someone walking out. He would never forget his father's face turning red as he tried to convince people that the IRA protesters were the villains. His parents had moved to provide a better future for their children. Gordon knew he would have done the same.

Chapter 6

August 15th
New York City, New York

James had arrived the previous morning from Bristol. Rested, but still suffering from jet lag, he rubbed his eyes, sat up on the bed and reached for his coffee cup. He had been awake since four a.m. He never looked forward to these monthly trips, even though he always stayed at a five star hotel. To him the island was an olfactory assault made up of too many people, exhaust fumes and unknown aromas from corner street vendors.

Preparing for his morning meeting, James organized his notes and his thoughts; standing in front of the board reporting results was never mentioned in the job description.

The trip across the street to the GeneQwest office on 4th street took him the better of five minutes. Dodging the yellow cabs, James crossed the street, pushed the revolving door and stood at the bank of elevators waiting to be whisked to the 33rd floor. The familiar ring indicated its arrival and within thirty seconds he was facing the smiling receptionist.

"Good morning Mr. Mitchell, back for your monthly meeting?"

"Yes, that's right Rebecca. Once a month is all I can handle," he said smiling.

"Head right in. They're expecting you," she said.

"Cheers." James headed for the boardroom. "Morning gentlemen," he said as he walked in.

He was armed with the latest findings from his research and ready for the typical barrage of questions from his undereducated bosses.

"Morning James," said Josh, sipping on his cappuccino.

"Want a coffee to start the morning off right?" asked Gordon.

"No, thanks, already had one. I was up early this morning," replied James.

Taking a seat at the middle at the table, he opened his laptop to start up his PowerPoint presentation.

"So, what's the good news? Research done and we can all retire to a life of luxury?" joked Gordon.

"Well maybe," James smiled back. "Depends on

what you want to retire with. Gentlemen, let me start this meeting with this month's discoveries." With a touch of the mouse, the presentation floated onto the wall screen. It had all the elements of a documentary with video, charts, graphs and numbers explained by a sophisticated voice over.

"Gordon, you see from the progress we've made that we are closer than ever to cracking the genetic code for the lung cancer cell. We have worked hard in obtaining these results and my team has put in an extraordinary effort to get to this point.

"I must note that there are other scientists and researchers attempting the same thing. I have heard that they are very close to cracking the genome for the same cell. It appears to me that GeneQwest is on the verge of a breakthrough. For you, gentlemen, this means the time is approaching when we will be able to go to market with a product to help humanity with this killer disease." James stopped to take a several sips from a glass of water.

"What is your time line on this release?" asked Josh.

"I think that if we estimate two months, that wouldn't be out of line," James replied.

"So from your presentation, when would you

recommend our first release to the media should be?" asked William.

"If we publish our findings on gene recognition, it would be significant. Patents and trademarks should be in place by then?" James asked Gordon.

"Absolutely," replied Gordon, leaning back in his chair, his hands linked on the back of his head.

"So according to our business plan, we make the announcement about how it relates to cancer, but how much money are we talking and what is our market share?" one of the board members inquired.

"Hard to quantify Stephen, but conservatively I would say four hundred million dollars, but that is just a guess. We market the drug to companies that presently sell the drugs to cancer patients, they will sell our product for us and we can work on isolating another gene for the market place," replied Gordon.

"I will talk to Jim and find out where we would have the least competition for the next one," said Stephen.

"Ok, I have a slight change of plan," said Gordon, "James, within the next few days you and your team will be receiving a sample that I would like you work on. It's a slight change in direction, but an important one for

GeneQwest. I am trying to get it to you before you head back to Bristol, but I'm not sure if I will get it by then. Either way, when you do get it, please start work immediately."

"Absolutely, Gordon. Can you tell me something about this sample?"

"Not yet James, you will see it soon enough," replied Gordon.

The other partners looked at each other wondering if either of them knew something the other did not.

Josh piped up, "Gordon, what is this all about? I thought we had a firm business plan in place. You never vary from it. What's going on?"

"Gentlemen, trust me on this one. I will let you know more very soon, just give me a week or so and I will fill you in. It will all work out for the best, actually even better than you think." Gordon pushed his chair back, preparing to stand up and end the meeting.

By evening, James was back at LaGuardia heading back to Bristol.

Chapter 7

Walking into the cavernous shell of the lab, James called out "Morning!" No one would be in yet, he just wanted to hear his voice bounce off the walls.

"Morning James," a voice echoed back.

Surprised and pleased to find some company, James headed in the direction of the voice.

In the corner with a desk light on over her computer was Sara.

"How was your trip to New York?" she asked.

"Same as it always is, report that everything is going according to Hoyle, chat up the board and then get back on the plane. Not very exciting I'm afraid. I see nothing has changed," James continued, "it seems it's always just you and me here in the morning."

"I know," replied Sara. "Seems to be a pattern developing here: both of us kick starting the lab and the rest of them strolling in looking for fresh coffee and a smile."

"How about today we switch it up?" asked James. "Interested in going for a coffee just down the road? Let's see how the rest of the team like coming in to an empty office. What do you think?"

"I think that's a brilliant idea," Sara smiled.

She liked having time alone with James. She could learn a lot by just being around him plus he was funny and somewhat handsome.

"I'm ready to go anytime you are," James said.

"Come on then, let's go just in case one of them shows up early."

Coat in hand James glanced at the hands of the old fashioned analog clock: 8:45. It was one hour before the rest of his team usually showed up. Waiting at the door he heard Sara's voice echo through the lab.

"I will be right there, sorry."

"No rush," he echoed in return.

The sharp ringing tone bounced of the lab walls. The doorbell caught James off guard. He turned and opened the door. A man in a brown uniform was smiling with a package in his hands.

"Morning, package for Illumina Labs, would that

be you?" he asked.

"That would be me."

"Just put your John Hancock right there and I will leave you in peace."

Electronic pen in hand, James signed for the lunch box sized brown box that was marked *Urgent, Fragile* and *Special Delivery*. He read the sender's label. *Andros Corporation, New Mexico, USA.*

Sara arrived ready to head for the coffee bar.

"Just delivered?"

"Yes. Come on, let's get that coffee, we can open it there."

Five minutes down the road tucked between the local bakery and stationary shop, Top Cup welcomed its usual morning crowd. Grabbing two coffees, James headed to the table that Sara had laid claim to.

"Come on then, open up the package," Sara said impatiently.

"Alright, let's have a go at this thing," James replied.

Looking for a corner to start unwrapping, James peeled away the brown paper to expose a letter taped to the top of the box that read "OPEN THIS FIRST."

Reaching into his pant pocket James pulled out his key ring with his house and bike key on it along with a small yellow pocket knife he used in emergencies. Slitting the blank number ten sized envelope with a clean cut, James pulled out the thick off-white paper. Opening up the folded single sheet, he immediately noticed the GeneQwest letterhead.

"So, what does it say?" asked Sara.

James quickly scanned the letter. "Hang on a sec and I will let you know."

The letter read:

James,

Enclosed is a sample uncovered in the hills of Montana by a little known subsidiary of GeneQwest, Andros Corp. We believe it to be of tremendous significance and I would like you to devote as much, if not all of your time to unlocking the secrets of this discovery. It is the unfossilized tissue of a T-Rex, the only one of its kind. This is a great find for GeneQwest and I trust you can see the value of any resulting research.

James, this is one for you and you only. I trust you will safeguard this information as all results will remain the property of GeneQwest and the announcement of any findings will be at my discretion. Good Luck."

Gordon Lynch
CEO, GeneQwest

"So, anything interesting?" asked Sara.

"I believe so. Let me have some time for this one to sink in. Good coffee here isn't it?" James said, trying unsuccessfully to change the subject.

Sara winced and looked up, wondering what she was missing out on.

"Yes, it is good," she said, staring right at James.

Chapter 8

November 25th

While the November rain pelted down outside, the team had their eyes glued to their screens, silent, focused and efficient, gathering the answers to the questions that James had fielded in his latest monthly meeting. The usual jovial atmosphere was replaced by the drumming of keyboards as they diligently created ammunition. They knew by now that on his return his requests for information increased and he became demanding and edgy until his jet lag had run its course a few days later.

"Good night James," said Peter, pulling his knapsack over one shoulder. "I'm off to the movies tonight, let you know tomorrow if it was any good," he said heading toward the door.

"Good night, thanks for your work today," James replied, "See you tomorrow"

"Yep, I'm out of here as well. Don't work too hard James," Sara said as she put on her raincoat.

"I won't. Do I ever?" smiled James.

"Yes, yes you do," she said, waving goodbye as she pushed the door open.

After everyone had gone home, James entered the workroom. He sat down at a table that served as the focal point for one quadrant of the lab. Hands on experiments were still essential even in a computer-driven laboratory. Organizing some papers on the edge of the table, he hooked his legs through the first rung on the stool and studied the assorted medical cutlery scattered between beakers of various sizes. It appeared some unusual experiment was taking place right on the table. Unlike James, neatness was not the group's forte.

Returning to his office he moved the mouse and his screen saver, a picture of a black swan morphing into a white swan, slowly disintegrated. With no one around to bother him, James turned the music off. Lukewarm coffee in hand, he began to relax and focus his thoughts, settling in for the evening.

He typed in his password and waited. When the "Open a File?" prompt popped up, he moved the cursor to the new folder and double clicked on the day's results.

Scrolling up and down through the pages, James reviewed the data.

With the team gone home for the day, the large echo chamber of a lab amplified every sound. James listened to the sporadic dripping from inside the old water pipes that hung overhead. The silence buzzed in his ears as he moved his chair closer to his computer and the two oversized computer screens became his canvas for mathematical art, both purring for his attention. His concentration increased with the solitude.

In the three months since the letter instructed him to devote his time to work exclusively on the tissue sample; his detective work had been focused on unlocking ancient DNA secrets left behind in a genetic time capsule. He had involved his team sparingly, limiting their knowledge of his work as part of the mandate from management. This project was for his eyes only.

The multi colored double helix twisted on the screen in slow motion. The familiar strands held the instructions for every living thing on earth, this one happened to be 65 million years old. The sample had been incubating in trypsin, a chemical inducer known to excite the IFN receptors provoking dormant genes to display their hidden genetic roadmap.

James sat glued to the monitor watching as the creature's DNA was revealed for the first time. The long nights of work had been worth it, his choice of Illumina vindicated. He felt a strange kind of guilt mixed with pride as the creature's most intimate secrets spun around on the screen. He became conscious of himself, alone, with knowledge that could change the world. The weight of responsibility came down like an anvil.

Staring at the swirling dinosaur DNA, James typed in a request for research results to compare the sequence of genes between recent mammoth samples and his own bit of T-Rex. The research was sitting in Cray supercomputers just down the darkened hall. The columns of ten sealed in the climate controlled glass enclosure talked between themselves. Within seconds one screen displayed the T-Rex genome and the other showed the mammoth. James mined the sequenced regions for similarities. The amino acids, proteins and RNA all matched, even the mutation in the string algorithm matched. He could not believe his eyes; in front of him was a fact that was undeniable and disturbing.

Further splitting the screen with the T-Rex DNA, he called up one more sample, human DNA from a recent brain cancer patient, a 52-year-old healthy male from Minnesota. The database showed that he had died within a month and had no previous symptoms. The three genetic maps spun in unison like a well-choreographed dance, all exhibiting the same results. Evolution had commandeered a voice. It was now unveiling its message: no species endures forever.

James could feel the rush of a new discovery running through his veins. The dopamine pumped around his body like a marathon runner's high. James walked around the lab, scratching his head and forearms, trying to control his agitation. He knew with certainty that he had made a breakthrough in genetics. He forced himself to remember to document it all: time of event, time of discovery, what equipment he was using, how strong a power was used for the electron microscope. How long had the tissue been in trypsin, what test trial led to the results? What was the temperature of the lab? Hundreds of questions raced through his mind. He took some time to catch his breath and calm down. He needed to gather his thoughts and get them down on paper, or at least type something to be stored on his computer.

For the next two hours he documented his procedures and results. He meticulously charted every test result and wrote down all the samples he had used before this one. Solid evidence was just as important as the conclusion. He finally typed the last line, hoping that he had thought of every question and variable that he would be asked. When he was confident that he could counter all opposition to his theory he ended the report.

He shoved all the paperwork into his briefcase, gathered all his post-it notes, anything that could lead someone to the same discovery he had just made. Before shutting down his computer he loaded a jump drive with all the information and any related documents. Then he wiped the computer files clean.

Looking at the clock he was amazed to see that it was now 10:30 and four hours had gone by. Pressing a sequence of numbers until the green light indicated he was correct, he activated the security system, turned the lights out, and pushed the main door open. The moist night air enveloped him as he turned and locked the door to the building.

He quickened his pace heading for the bike stand. He hitched his knapsack, checking that it was securely attached to his back, rolled up his beige pants so they didn't get caught in the chain and pedaled to the garage door, then headed north on Wine Street and turned at the next corner in the direction of his apartment. He felt his nervous energy changing into paranoia. No one else knew what he knew, no one could figure it out, he reassured himself.

Maybe a quick Guinness would help calm him down. He decided to drop into the pub for one drink before last call.

James chained his bike to the rusted bike stand outside the pub. At this point in the evening he thought it was better to lock it up than risk losing it to some drunk. He unrolled his pant leg from his sock, trying to straighten his creased pants as he walked, and pushed the wooden door open to enter The Hatchet Inn. Once inside, his casual shirt and out of style trousers blended easily with the local crowd and he felt a sense of relief. The familiar pub where he had enjoyed a game of darts with his fellow workers felt like a second home to him now even though he rarely went there anymore.

James found a seat by the fireplace where a cheerful blaze was keeping out the November chill. Blowing into his hands to get some warmth and circulation going after the bike ride he barely had a chance to sit down before he heard someone shout his name.

"James!"

He glanced around in the direction of the voice.

"James, over here," called a waving Sara.

James headed over to where she sat at a table full of empty beer glasses. It was clear that Sara and her girlfriends had had a few pints.

"Girls, this is James Mitchell. He is our leader, our top dog, our big boss."

"Ok, that's enough, I work with Sara, that's all," James interrupted, blushing.

"So what's the occasion?" Sara asked.

"What do you mean, occasion?" replied James.

"Well you know, it isn't too often I see you here this late, must be a reason?"

"No reason really," said James.

Sara turned her head and smiled, "Come on, you can tell me, can't you?"

"Just needed something to calm the nerves, and I can see that you are very calm," James said smiling.

"Calm, yes, I am very calm. In fact I am past calm."

"Well that's good. Nice to see you're enjoying yourself."

"Yep, I definitely am doing that. Along with a few of my gal pals we have beaten that dart board to death," she said, pointing to the pitted board.

"Looks like you missed a few," said James dryly.

"Just a few," laughed Sara, "So what can I get you James?"

"Thanks Sara, but let me get this one?"

"Ok, I won't say no to that," Sara laughed again and watched James head for the bar.

A minute later he was back with two pints in hand. As he passed one to Sara he noticed that her friends had moved on to the dartboard. Carefully moving his briefcase from under his arm to the seat beside him, he settled into the booth.

"Cheers," said James, raising his pint.

Sara did the same. "So did you figure out that problem you were showing me today? I'm telling you I couldn't see it. Are you sure you aren't just dreaming this thing?" Sara said putting her hand on James' shoulder.

"Nope, it's there, that's why I am enjoying this pint. It's kind of a celebration," James said as he took a big swallow of the black beer.

"Well that's great! Want to fill me in a bit?"

"Ok, I can give you some idea, but the computer shows it better. It looks like you won't remember in the morning if I told you anyway!" joked James.

"Great, let's hear it."

James moved closer to Sara, to protect the information from too many people, but he quickly realized that not one person in the pub would have the faintest clue what he was talking about. He hesitated, remembering Gordon's instructions, but the urge to share his discovery was overwhelming and he suddenly realized that of all the people in the lab, Sara was the person that he trusted the most.

"I'll fill you in, but you have to know that this information is strictly confidential. Gordon doesn't even know about this yet and there could be some consequences if it gets out. Do I have your word that you won't share this with anyone?"

"James, you can count on me. Not a word of this will be repeated to anyone, I swear. Now tell me," Sara said solemnly.

"Well, you know we have been looking at the double helixes from countless samples, experimenting with various combinations of amino acids with proteins. Tonight I saw one that had paired with the junk DNA that we figured was useless to us. But here is the kicker: when provoked it launched into - well, hard to name it - but I would say that it was programmed sudden death. It basically self-destructed."

Sara took another swallow of her beer while looking at James

"What...What the hell are you talking about? That's nuts. That would be absolutely counter-intuitive to all natural things. It would be programmed suicide for a species."

"I know, but it gets worse. I was comparing was the skin tissue we got from those guys in Montana to some human DNA from a donor who had brain cancer and they were the same."

"What? Hold it," said Sara, "Are you telling me that from what you saw on the screen... dinosaurs basically committed suicide?"

"Well I don't know if you would call it suicide. I figure they didn't have any choice; what took them out was their own DNA. It was their pre-programmed time to go. Their time was up."

Sara went silent, struggling to figure out if James had gone crazy or if all the beer she had consumed had finally kicked in.

"And now you're saying you see the exact same thing in us? Come on James, stop messing around. That is just crazy."

"It may sound batty, but tomorrow when we are back at the lab I'll show you on the screen. You can see for yourself."

"That is one hell of a thing, what you're talking about. Let's hope you're wrong."

"We can run more tests tomorrow to verify what I saw, but my gut tells me I'm right."

Sara and James sat back, beers in hand, both draining their glasses at the same time.

"So I tell you what, let's call it a night, regroup in the morning after I recuperate and then check out your findings," said Sara.

"Sounds good, let's head out. I need some time to think," James replied.

"Right then James, I'll see you tomorrow." Sara got up and waved to her friends who were still butchering the dartboard. She motioned that she needed to get home.

Within five minutes the group had packed up and jammed into the Vauxhall sitting outside the pub. Sara leaned her head on the window in the back seat. She was in no condition to drive.

Ten minutes later she was asleep in her bed.

James unlocked his bike and started to pedal

home, five minutes up the road. A light rain had started, the streetlights reflected off the wet streets. The cool evening wind picked up and made his ride home more uncomfortable. He considered a change in transportation.

As James turned the key in the door of his apartment, back at the lab the network computer began its nightly backup.

Chapter 9

Sara was the first one in the lab next morning. She made coffee and headed for her station, booted up her computer and waited for the familiar screen prompt, *password please.*

Within an hour everyone was in the lab, hard at work.

James walked in looking haggard from the night before, but with some enthusiasm still in his eyes.

"Morning all," he said. His voice was just a bit louder than usual.

"Morning James," like a choir his team chirped in unison.

"So James, how was the rest of your evening?" asked Sara.

"Well, there wasn't much of the evening left by the time we left the pub, but I did have some time this morning riding my bike here and…" James smiled and raised his eyebrow in acknowledgement of success.

Sara headed directly over to James after the inference of victory. She followed him into his office walking closely behind him and closing the door after herself.

"Are you kidding?" said Sara, "So you weren't jerking my chain last night?"

"Would I do that to you Sara?" James said with a hurt tone in his voice.

"So you were telling me the truth?" asked Sara, perplexed.

"Yes, of course I was," he replied.

"Well, can we see what all the fuss is about then?" smiled Sara.

"Ok, well that might be a problem. The "we" part anyway. Remember that letter I opened a while back, the one that came along with the package?"

"Yep, I remember."

"Well, there was a reference, or an implied one anyway, that I had to be careful about sharing the results and so far, last night was the first time I had even told anyone."

"Ok, I guess I should feel privileged," Sara said, placing her hand over her heart.

"Sort of I guess, but I still think you should have a look at the findings. You know as well as I do validation of results is everything. Come and have a look but remember what you promised last night."

James motioned to Sara to sit in his chair to get a better view of the screen displays. He loaded the jump drive and the three images appeared in front of Sara.

"So watch this area right here." James pointed to the screen. "See the similarities? It's eerie, to use a technical term," James smiled.

Sara stared at the screens before answering; she knew enough to understand the comparables.

"Well, I do like your terminology, eerie is right, but I would add scary. This can only lead to one conclusion."

"Yes, it appears that we are going to be joining the legions of other extinct species that have left this planet. Our time is up."

Sara's face stiffened, paralyzed by James's statement. She paused before responding.

"James, are we really witnessing our impending death?"

"I think we are witnessing our planned obsolescence. Natural evolution has won for millions of years and it will win again."

"I can't believe that. There must be a way of changing it, something in the DNA we can shift or remove. Do we just sit back and watch it happen?"

"We will know soon I think. It happened pretty quickly to the dinosaurs."

"James, we have to do something."

"Well, at this point I don't know what that is."

Chapter 10

October 7th

James eyed the DNA double helix spinning on his computer screen in an attempt to see something that he had not seen before. If the answer was in front of him it would just be a matter of time, he hoped. Sometimes if he stared at something long enough the synapses in his brain would finally kick in and lead him to the answer. He often used this technique when faced with molecular problems. This time the DNA strand in the multi-coloured computer model spun endlessly without revealing its secret.

Next to his computer was his notebook. As his ideas flowed from his brain to his fingers, he jotted them down. He didn't like to use his computer for thinking things through. The old method worked faster; an HB pencil and a spiral notebook were his weapons of choice. Page after page of random thoughts were transformed into reasonable formulas on the lined paper. At the top of the first page was the heading, underlined and capitalized, "Theoretical solution to mutating junk DNA."

The well thumbed, coffee stained pages full of underlined passages, arrows and circled words were the result of the last four months of work. The struggle to find a solution for the mutation's effect on humans weighed heavily on him. He was expected to lead the development team in finding a solution. He knew the secret would be part of a business proposal being optioned out to the highest bidder, probably a large pharmaceutical firm. Without a doubt it would make them all millionaires, but more importantly he needed to find a cure.

Books in alphabetical order stood straight in the brushed metal bookcase. James walked along tapping his pencil on the spines of the assorted scientific publications. Sharing shelf space with the likes of Jay Gould and biographies of Watson and Crick was his prized possession, a fourth edition of *On the Origin of Species* by Charles Darwin. Pulling down the well-used book, he thumbed through it, getting a whiff of the familiar old pages.

Returning to his computer, its screen still spinning the double helix, he moved the wireless mouse to start again. He needed to wrestle a retrovirus into existence that would defeat the mutant gene that was slowly taking away all of mankind's options. Needing Darwin's words close by for encouragement James positioned the book not far from his computer. The dichotomy of old and new was not lost on him. Darwin had discovered the mutations that were needed for evolution; he was working to keep mankind evolving.

With a double click the program displayed the 3D model of the molecular break-up of the DNA into RNA, the messenger code of life's instructions provided to every cell. As a routine check, he reexamined the T-Rex's code for the deadly gene about to cause havoc in the world's population. Alone at the desk he watched the program execute the helper cells as they become infected with the new killer virus. The structural change to the DNA of the tissue sample displayed the peculiar characteristics that had spelled the demise of the dinosaur. The nucleus of the T-Rex contained a gene that told the organism to turn off its biological clock and stop replicating. Death was just a matter of time. The program went through its algorithms to display how the RNA produced a different set of instructions to create the destructive new DNA. One protein roamed up and down the DNA looking for an entry point to change the amino acids that modified the DNA, creating the time bomb.

James noted a consistent pattern to the protein's behaviour. The key lay in changing the behaviour of the amino acid forcing it to stop its destructive work. All this had to take place in the junk DNA that James knew was still a mystery to geneticists. But the answer was in the junk.

The second hand on the wall clock ticked silently along its white face, seconds adding to minutes, adding to hours. It was a long time before James got up from his chair. His legs were hurting where they met the edge of his chair; the lack of leg movement had stiffened his quads. He stood up to stretch both his legs and arms to restore his circulation.

Studying the molecular model reminded him of why he had chosen the field in the first place: Life on earth was nothing but molecules arranged in the right genetic order to follow instructions. His task now was to rearrange the molecules that had gone rogue. Complex as they were, James knew that like puzzles, there was always a solution: the thousand-piece puzzle ended up as one big picture. He knew the answer was floating around in his cranium; he just had to mine it out. The RNA knew what it had to do, the DNA followed the instructions. James had to tap into the DNA and reverse its interpretation of the rules. The computer program would help to mimic the genetic process and model the changes, display the results, list the findings and then try again.

Anticipating the multitude of options the program had yet to run, he left it churning away as he packed up for the night. The morning would bring him some more results, and then he could interpret the findings.

Threading his arms through his Gortex jacket, he grabbed his bike from its inside parking spot and headed for the front entrance. The night had not only brought on the darkness, but had also provided a blanket of fog to cover the city. Night time pedaling was not a favorite activity for James. Arming himself with strategically placed yellow reflector stickers that he kept in his under-seat satchel, he turned his front wheel to avoid the curb and ventured on to the old road scattered with potholes of assorted sizes, all waiting to trip up unsuspecting cyclists. The usual thirty-minute ride became a cautious forty-five minute test of survival.

Arriving safely at his apartment, James chained his bike to the side of the building alongside the bikes of other environmentally-conscious tenants and headed up to his flat. Inside James switched on the television to hear the BBC nightly news before heading off to bed.

"Good evening, this is Harry Thorens with the latest news," echoed through the room.

"Good Morning, this is Lara Gilbert with the morning news."

James woke on the sofa to the combined sounds of BBC and the telephone. He had no memory of falling asleep. After three annoying rings he found the phone.

Through the rain-stained window of his apartment the sun streaked in, laying separate beams of yellow light on the hardwood floor and warming the room. The wall clock held its arms up at ten o'clock. Rubbing the sleep from his tired eyes, James headed for the coffee maker; he needed a caffeine charge today.

"Hello," he answered still feeling dazed and confused.

"Morning James," a female voice resonated through the phone, "Are you coming in this morning?"

"Sara?" he questioned.

"Yes, it's me, just ringing you to see if you are coming in?" Sara asked.

"What time is it?" James asked as he glanced at

the clock. "Shit, is that ten o'clock?"

"Yes...it's ten. Are you alright, what happened?" asked Sara.

"Nothing, just can't believe I slept in. Ten o'clock, shit, I can't remember the last time I did that," James replied, still in a fog.

"Are you sure you're ok?"

"Yes, yes, I'm fine, just have to get my head in gear that's all. I'll be in soon."

"Ok, well your computer has been running all night. Did you know that?"

Like a mental reboot, he played back his memories of the night before at the lab.

"Yes, I remember now. I left it on as I wanted to let it do some number crunching. Is it still working?" asked James.

"Well, it's on, and I think it has done whatever you wanted because I don't hear anything from the CPU," Sara said.

"Ok, then just leave it and I'll be in soon, maybe in an hour or so. See you soon."

"Ok, see you then," Sara said and hung up.

James sat at the kitchen table, one leg tucked around the leg of the chair. He slowly collected his thoughts.

Half an hour later he was dressed and on his bike heading to the lab. The sun was out for the day with no clouds in sight. It would be a splendid day in Bristol.

Passing the usual haunts, his late morning ride provided him with glimpses of people who were usually still asleep when he rode by at dawn. With winter around the corner, final grooming was in full swing. People were tending their small gardens outside attached houses, an army of retirees enjoying their earned time off.

His rhythmic pedaling floated him through the calm surroundings. Taking in the scenery, relaxed and alert, he passed by one grey haired man fine tuning his already perfect hedge. At that moment James knew what the answer was. He followed the motion of the clippers on the green branches. He coasted for a moment as his mind focused on the image that had passed before him on the screen the night before. Then his wheels turned faster and faster as he dodged the left over puddles and lurking pot holes and weaved his two-wheeler through the narrow streets until he saw the door of the lab. As he approached, he dismounted, glided the short distance left, wheeled his bike through the door, dropped it and headed to the now dormant computer.

A faint chorus of greetings registered with him as he pulled his wheeled chair closer to the computer. Lighting the screen with a jab to the return key, the numbers and colorful graphic appeared. Scrolling down the screen searching for confirmation of his bike ride epiphany, his mind raced along with page after page that appeared and disappeared as fast as he could manage. Faster and faster, the scrolling motion pushed the pages through like a printing press at high speed. Getting closer to where he needed to be, James slowed the process, looking at each page with more interest.

"James, good morning, would you like some help with something?" said Sara from his office doorway.

"What? No, I'm good," James said not really paying attention.

Ok, well if you do, let me know."

"I will, sure, I will," James said hurriedly.

Slowing down, the screen stopped its unraveling like a slot machine with the winning combination. James leaned forward and studied the results. There in front of him was the answer and he stared at the solution in reverence. Line by line James read every result in concert with the 3D graphic, spinning in front of him was the RNA claw clipping the strand and replacing the broken

DNA with its destructive amino acid to produce the time bomb DNA.

He knew what to do. He allowed himself a small grin. He had solved the thousand-piece puzzle.

Pushing back from his desk, he replayed the 3D animation again and again, watching the molecular break-up create its killer DNA, the lobster styled claw chomping down on its prey and sending in the intruder. What he had to do now was to nullify the retrovirus by replacing the killer with a pacifist.

Passing by his office, Sara noticed a more relaxed James leaning back. She poked her head into see if he was in a better mood.

"So, Mr. James, are you back with us?"

"Yes, sorry about that, but I had to make sure my hypothesis was correct. You know how it is when you get something in your head and you don't want it to leave?"

"Yep, sure do, so what was stuck in there?" Sara said pointing to his head.

"Come over and take a look."

Sara came around the desk. Looking at the screen she saw the graphic spinning repeatedly, biting down on the DNA.

"Ok, I see it, what are we looking at?"

"We are watching a latent gene modifying the molecular make up of a DNA strand; we are watching molecular intelligence at work. Somehow these amino acids have been told to change the strand. What would make them do that? I'm not sure why, but I know how to change it. Do you know what that means?" asked James.

"It means that we can change that behaviour, it means we can control what they do, or at least stop them," Sara replied.

"That's right, and can we use this to stop a cancer, because the cells keep growing no matter what we do to them? I'm not sure yet, but I see another application for this."

"What application, can I ask?" queried Sara

"Right now, Sara, I can't tell you, but I will. I have to run a few more scenarios to confirm my theory, but I'm confident that I'm right."

"Ok, well when you do, let me in on it will you?"

"Yes, I will, you'll be the first to know."

"Ok, want to get some lunch?"

"Lunch already?"

"Well some of us were here at eight this morning," smiled Sara.

"Right, ok, I am getting a bit peckish. Meet you at

the front door in five minutes."

Walking out of James' office Sara knew it would be more than five minutes.

Gordon's Blackberry rung with the familiar tone signaling the arrival of an email. Sitting at his oversized desk, Gordon reached for the device to see who had sent it.

He had been in the office for two hours and another caffeine hit was required. He decided to get his coffee before he opened the email. He returned to his chair, sipping his refill before putting his cup down. Email from James was usually an update on progress or notification of his travel plans. Gordon pressed the middle button and opened the email. The time sent indicated that James was working late, very late. With a quick calculation, Gordon realized it was well past midnight in Bristol.

Gordon, thought you should know. I have addressed your request to turn the antidote into a powdered substance. If your goal was to provide a pill to individuals, I believe that this is what you've asked for.

Realizing James had just sent it Gordon replied immediately.

Thank you James, I will fill you in on the application when I'm up next week in Bristol. This will benefit many people. Excellent work.

James saw Gordon's reply arrive, quickly read it and then turned his phone off and headed home.

Chapter 11

With Christmas passed, the amount of packages handled by Vatican staff was finally waning. Deliveries to various church officials always exceeded staff capacity.

The nondescript brown parcel had been precisely placed in the centre of the Pope's desk. It had been scanned, x-rayed and tested for all the various potential explosive devices and biological threats that might be found in a package sent to the Vatican.

The Pope usually reviewed the day's agenda with his two secretaries after celebrating mass and taking his early morning breakfast meeting. This morning he was there long before they were due to arrive. He walked down the marble hallway into his office and pulled the door closed behind him.

His large wooden desk sat bathed in sunlight from the windows that overlooked St. Peter's square. He took a moment to glance out over the familiar scene in the plaza where a few families were feeding pigeons and tourists were snapping photos. Walking over to his desk, past the bookcase full of theological treatises, he pulled back his chair and sat down, dragging the package towards him.

The box had been neatly opened. He only had to reach in to lift out the bound, bubble-wrapped document. An envelope, slit open by security, was still taped by its four corners to the bubble wrap. He tore the envelope off, taking small pieces of the cover with it. He picked up an opener with the papal crest of a gold and silver key and hesitated, unexpectedly remembering the scripture that ruled his whole life. *"You are Peter, and upon this rock I will build my church, and the gates of hell shall not prevail against it. I will give you the keys to the kingdom of heaven. Whatever you bind on earth shall be bound in heaven; and whatever you loose on earth shall be loosed in heaven."*

He bowed his head for a moment, and then pulled the letter out. Folding back the single thick page he began to read.

Your Holiness,

Thank you for accepting this letter and the accompanying

documents which have been delivered through somewhat unorthodox channels. The reason for this will become clear as you read the material. This is a matter of the greatest urgency and we would like to make clear the gravity of the situation, the full consequences and the ramifications of your decision. I trust you will engage with us in further conversation after a full review of our proposal.

> *Regards,*
> *Gordon Lynch*
> *CEO, GeneQwest Corp.*

Placing the letter on the desk he wondered if he should just seal the box back up and never look at it again. He did not want to do something that could not be undone, and he knew that some things were better left in the hands of God.

He walked around his desk rearranging the pens and papers. His nerves occasionally got the better of him and he had a habit of rearranging things that didn't need arranging. He had now completely rearranged his desk.

The tightly bound one hundred page document rested on the desk. He cracked the binding open to lay it flat and turned to the first page of the document. It had no title, but despite that it had his complete attention. He began to read, pushing his glasses up from their balancing point near the end of his nose.

In the world today, he read, there are companies working within the boundaries of the accepted norm and solving problems in conventional ways. GeneQwest is not one of those companies. We are and always have been a leader in the world of pharmaceuticals and genetics. It is in the spirit of leadership that I would like to present our business proposal. At our research labs in Bristol, England, GeneQwest has made a discovery that will change the lives of millions and will provide a unique opportunity to a select group of people around the globe. As you may know, the main thrust of our work has been in comparative genomics. This line of research works with the DNA strands that provide each of us with our distinct characteristics. This research has now enabled GeneQwest to offer the Catholic Church one of the greatest opportunities in history.

We are willing to provide Your Holiness with irrefutable scientific proof that will restore the Catholic religion to its rightful place among world religions. It will position Catholicism as the only true faith for everyone on Earth. It is nothing less than the confirmation of the truth that God has selected the Catholics of the world to be His chosen ones. If, as we believe, God has decided to select one religion to follow for salvation, then all eyes will turn to the Roman Catholic Church, and to you, Your Holiness, to provide the ultimate message from our heavenly Father.

GeneQwest trusts that you will consider the following

proposal as the only viable choice that can be made with good conscience for the sake of human beings everywhere.

The entire research is described in the following pages where you will find that we can provide the Church with the means to become the most dominant religion ever known to mankind. Indeed, it will be the only option.

One hour later he had finished the brief.

Leaning back, he pushed the book away, removed his reading glasses and started chewing one of the arms. He stared without seeing at the dark paneled bookcase, then turned his gaze away and positioned his head in the palms of his hands. He could not believe what he had just read. He slumped in the chair, wishing that he could disappear. There was a knock on the door. The Pope regained his composure and picked up his pen, pretending to look over some paperwork.

"Your Holiness," said his secretary as he opened the heavy door and moved into the room.

"Yes?" replied the Pope.

"Cardinal Howard is here for his appointment."

"Yes, show him in."

He covered the book with other papers and prepared for the Cardinal's presence, even though he was preoccupied with the words he had just read. After fifteen minutes of discussion that he could barely comprehend and would never remember, the Cardinal left and the Pope returned to his desk, pushed the camouflaging pagers off the top of the document and opened it to the final pages. He reread the conclusion one more time. It became apparent that the decision would not be an easy one. He would have to make inquiries at the Pontifical Academy of Sciences and then, if what he read was true, he would need the best minds of the church to help him decide.

Although it was not spelled out, there was no doubt that the information that GeneQwest was offering would undoubtedly lead to a worldwide stampede to the Catholic faith, easily bringing the number of faithful up from one billion to four billion or more. The idea of leading the world to the light of God was tempting, but of course there was a catch – a catch that would be spelled out by GeneQwest's representative if he decided to meet with him. And of course, the veiled threat was the implication that they could offer the same information to any other religious leader who was willing to meet their price.

The Pope sat in the ornate red velvet upholstered

chair reading the latest numbers from the Vatican accountants. It was not one of his favorite things to do, but simply one of the many intricacies of the job he was burdened with. Today he was reading with more than his usual interest. The heavy red drapes hardly moved as the air from the door pushed across the room. Pope John glanced above his reading glasses to see who had entered the room.

"Good morning your Holiness, you wanted to talk to me regarding an urgent matter?" Father Bernard said, looking agitated. He unconsciously rubbed his hands together to create some heat. He always felt cold in the marble chambers.

"Yes Bernard, that is correct."

Bernard was no longer a young man from Belfast. His years at the Vatican had given him many opportunities and finally the great honor of serving the Holy Father but his youth had slipped away leaving lines and creases in his face and hands. He lived to serve. His faith had never faded; in fact it was stronger as he neared the peak of his career. Now, at 68, his slightly hunched posture and restless arthritic hands made him look a few years older than he was.

"I am at your disposal your Holiness," Bernard

whispered.

The Pope sat at his desk surrounded by papers and his collection of crucifixes. Some were made of solid gold, presents from world leaders; some were simple wood carvings from Africa. His favorite was a gift from a former businessman who had turned to the priesthood late in life. It had a prominent position on his desk.

The Pope pushed back from his desk and stood up. "Bernard," he said, "Prepare yourself. We have a lot of work to do."

Chapter 12

Living in Rome was one thing, but working for the Vatican Academy of Sciences was another. Since being nominated by the Dean at Trinity College in Dublin and accepting her post ten years ago, Heather Duncan had been living her dream. Her nomination to the Academy had changed her life.

Rome was so different from Dublin. She loved learning Italian and relished the small shocks of cultural differences and the nuances of life in the shadow of the Vatican. The Italian lifestyle was second nature to her now.

At 35, Heather was dedicated to her research in genetic development and the adaptability of early embryonic life. Being part of a dynamic team offered her a platform to demonstrate her expertise as well as remaining on the cutting edge of genetic science. Three members of the team had been working with her since her early years, two others had recently joined. Team leader Enncio Monteleone had been part of the Academy for over twenty years, having recently taken the helm for this initiative; the whole team worked well together and had made important discoveries along the way. Life for Heather could not have been better, until she received a call from Enncio three weeks ago.

"Good morning Heather, Enncio here. Can you spare a half hour or so?"

"Good morning. Sure, I guess so. Is there a problem?" asked Heather.

"No, none whatsoever, I just need to talk to you about some developments that have come up. It is all good," Enncio replied in his thick Italian accent.

"Ok. You're in your office right?"

"Yes, can you see me waving to you?"

"Yes," she said with a laugh, "I'll be right over."

The large area dedicated to the team and their research had a main area with multiple computers in the middle and a few offices around the edge with floor to ceiling glass walls. Heather could see Enncio waving as she put the phone back on its base.

She threaded her way through other team

members who were staring at reports from the previous night. Standing in front of Enncio's office, she tapped lightly on his door to announce her arrival.

"Come in my dear, no need to knock, you know you can just walk in," Enncio said smiling.

The term of endearment was something that Heather was used to in Rome. It was now part of her overall understanding of Italian men.

"What's up?" asked Heather.

"Well, nothing is really up. Just wanted to let you know what is happening around here."

"Ok. Is there something going on that's different than any other day?"

"Well, let me just say that we have had a request for your services for another task, a very important one at that. You should be flattered my dear."

"Why don't you tell me and then I will figure out whether I'm going to be flattered or not?" smiled Heather.

"The world is in some need of help. It seems that there is a need for us to participate in some new research and you, Heather, have been invited to join the team that will be dedicated to finding the solution."

"Well, in that case I guess I am flattered, Enncio.

Do you know who requested me specifically?"

"All I know is that it came from one of the Cardinals. I am not sure which one; I was just instructed to inform you of the request."

"So, where does all this take place and when?"

"It is to take place right here, on the second floor, and it will start tomorrow."

"Really, that fast! What about all the things I have on the go right now?"

"I will take care of them, don't worry about that," said Enncio. "I will let you know the rest as soon as I get the green light on the specifics later today."

"Ok, well I'll just wrap up a few things before I relocate," said Heather, puzzled but delighted.

"Yes, my dear, good idea, I will let you know as soon as I know."

Heading back to her computer station, Heather wondered why she had been singled out to join the team. For the next couple of hours she concentrated on wrapping up her research in such a way that it would be clear to Enncio where she was in her attempts to identify the development of the totipotent potential of recombined embryos and their genetic material. While working on her documentation, she kept waiting for his phone call. When the phone finally rang, she pounced on it.

"Ok Heather, I have more details, can you come into my office and we will go over the information I have? Then you can head upstairs for the rest of the briefing."

"Yes, I'll be right there."

During her briefing with Enncio he elaborated on the process involved in the research, where it was taking place and who was running it. He also identified some other scientists that would be part of the team. Heather didn't recognize any of them.

"Ok Heather, there you have it, all the information that I have is now with you. Do you have any questions?"

"I do have one."

"Go ahead my dear, let me hear it."

"Well, if we do find the solution to this significant problem, do you know where it goes from there? I mean it will have global impact. Who actually owns "it" Enncio? Are we being sponsored by someone?"

"I don't know the answer to that, and I doubt I will be able to find out. There are others at work that will handle all that I assume. Our job, well, your job, will be to find out how to mitigate this thing. It is very important work, probably the most important work you will ever do, so I suggest you figure it out and let's see where the bocce ball rolls."

"Ok, I guess you're right. Thanks Enncio."

"No problem my dear, no problem at all," Enncio said, holding his palms out with a smile.

Chapter 13

February 17th
Vatican City, Italy

The upheaval started early the following day. A team of scientists, geneticists and biologists from various departments in the Academy were plucked from their research projects and herded together on the second floor of the historic Vatican Academy of Science. Combined with the six brought in from various corners of the world, the total was twenty people now dedicated to solving the mystery of the MG-J12 gene and unlocking its secretive codes.

The second floor arrangement for the incoming team had started at midnight the day before. Rearranging equipment, desks, and computers had left the floor in disarray. When the team arrived the following morning it was plain to everyone that there was still a lot of work to be done.

"Good morning all," said Cameron Kershaw, "I

am your team leader, and before we go any further, I first want to thank you for accepting the challenge at hand and I personally want to let you know that I look forward to working together with everyone and solving the mystery confronting us. Now I know that sounds corny, but I really mean it. Ok, now that that's out of the way, I suppose you're all wondering what we are going to do, how we are going to do it, and who is doing what. Well, I have the answers to all of those questions, and since we are not quite ready to begin, as you can see from this mess around you, let's head to the conference room and start the process. I think that area is almost complete and it will be away from all the commotion." Cameron pointed down the corridor.

Cameron Kershaw was an unknown quantity to the entire team of scientists who walked to the conference room like a line of school children after recess. As they would soon learn, he was the former head of the Academy's fund raising division, skilled in securing much-needed donations and gifts from Catholic organizations all over the world. His ability to persuade people to help the Church was unprecedented even though his flamboyant style sometimes crossed lines that the Vatican felt shouldn't necessarily be crossed. In his opinion, as the salesman for the Vatican, sometimes you had to shake things up. He thought of himself as a cultural liaison between the Church and its secular supporters. He had been appointed team leader by the president of the Pontifical Academy of Sciences following a direct request from the Pope, not for his medical expertise but because he was someone who could step aside from all things technical and focus on the task at hand - managing egos and expectations. Most importantly to His Holiness, Cameron's loyalty to the Holy Father was ironclad.

In the conference room, twenty scientists were crammed into an undersized area, all waiting on his words. Cameron stood at the head of the table, his back to the newly installed whiteboard, waiting for everyone to be comfortable. He glanced down at his Rolex watch and waited for the minute hand to hit the six on the dial. He started the meeting exactly on time.

"So, as you can see we have the table but no chairs," Cameron said, "but they are coming. The crew will be working all night to get everything in place and ready for us.

"I'm sure you know why we're here. We have been tasked to find the solution - the remedy or whatever you want to call it - to the biggest problem that mankind has ever faced. I know you are all aware of MG-J12 and how it is moving around the planet, so I won't get into unnecessary details, but we have to find a way of disarming it or eliminating it.

"How are we going to do that? Well, we have a plan, and to begin with, each of you standing here today will be tasked with a different aspect of the puzzle. This selection has been based on what each of you does best. We will then get together and discuss our findings. This will be a collaborative effort; no secrets, no keeping information away from someone else, it will be wide open and basically that is why I am here. My job is to make sure we get the most out of you. Let's put that another way," he said smiling, "My job is to help each of you with any request you have. I will do everything I possibly can to make your lives easier so we can get to that answer.

"Finally, when? Well, if I told you we needed the answer yesterday you would know what our timeline is. The short answer is right now.

"I would like to bring to your attention a few things of importance that I will assume we will all engage in. First off, communications: we will be the focus of media from around the world, so please do not talk or text anything to anyone without informing me - in fact, I would prefer that you do not engage anyone outside at all during your tenure here. Please let me do the talking and you do what you are here to do. No distractions, no interface with the press. Is that clear to everyone?"

Nodding heads indicated to Cameron to move on to the next point.

"When you return to your offices you will find 3D models of the DNA in question. Your task area will be defined and your collaborator will be named as well. That person will have access to your information and you to theirs; this is in the event of an unfortunate accident or sickness, and to mitigate any losses.

"You will also notice that the model will have areas of interest that we have no one assigned to as of yet. This will be an ongoing process as we get closer to the solution. Color coded areas of interest will either be removed as we find the solution to each or increased in importance if we discover that to solve one part we will need the answer in those areas.

"The DNA models have been obtained from various sample donors from around the world. They are indicative of the stages of this mutant gene; each will have a background dossier attached. We have over two thousand samples, so we have a good cross section to work with. Are there any questions?" Cameron's tone was all business now. "If there is anything that you can think of moving forward, please don't hesitate to let me know. My job here is to make your job painless; it is your experience and brainpower that we are counting on.

"There you have it people, a dedicated team with one goal, the best brains put to the ultimate test, saving mankind from extinction. Couldn't get any bigger. Your offices are posted on the floor plan on the wall just outside. Shall we get to work?"

Feeling the vibration of his phone through his pant pocket, Cameron pulled out his Blackberry and stepped to a quiet corner of the conference room. The group shuffled out into the hallway in search of their new offices. Heading to their new homes, they quickly engaged their computers and searched the DNA model looking for their assigned sections.

Answering his vibrating phone he spoke quieter than usual.

"Yes, all will be ready. It went well, a few blank stares but besides that nothing to worry about. Sorry can you repeat that?" Cameron asked.

Listening closely to caller, he replied, "It will not be a problem. I can assure you, we will be working in confidence, there will be no leaks, and the world will only hear what we want to release. Right, ok, I will keep you informed of any issues." Cameron finished the call by pressing end on his cell phone.

Across the courtyard Pope John slid his cell phone under his vestments and into his pants pocket. Finished with the matter at hand he returned to his meeting place to greet another world leader who had flown in carrying salutations and congratulations on his recent election.

Heather found her new office located close to the research hub area but far enough away to create some privacy for her to concentrate. It was the first time she had had an office and she inspected it with delight. Everything was in place, both computers hooked up and booted up. As soon as she moved the mouse, it revealed Heather's area in the junk DNA section.

She noticed Phillip Arevalo, the famous genetic biologist from France, across the hall and made a mental note to touch base with him soon.

She began to work. The hum of people resettling circled the room. An hour later the sound had diminished as the group focus turned to the task at hand.

Two weeks later the constant work had left the team members exhausted and at times short-tempered. Long hours and sore eyes became the norm. It was evident that Heather's task was not going to have an easy solution. Days and nights of concentrated effort went by before there were any signs of a breakthrough.

Dr. Fredrick Rocha, a staff Academy scientist, had discovered that the breakdown of a certain amino acid, once modified, affected other amino acids to produce a combatant gene, a battler to fight the mutant gene. There were positive results from preliminary testing, but after more trials it was revealed that the mutant gene would reassemble itself and kill the new gene attackers. It was the first of many false starts.

Chapter 14

A cool morning wind swirled around the bottom of the Pope's vestments as he crossed the courtyard. Overcast grey skies added nothing to the day. Before the tourists were allowed in he relished a walk to his office undisturbed.

In the corners of the courtyard stood the Swiss Guard in their orange and blue uniforms, on alert at all times protecting the Pope. Military trained sharpshooters dressed in costume party attire, they had been part of the Vatican chemistry for centuries. They watched as the Pope crossed the Pigna courtyard around the museum towards to the Belvedere courtyard. When he reached the Apostolic Building that housed his office, the guards stood down, but still stayed on alert as he reached for the handle and pushed the door open.

Lorenzo Corsini, the 268th Pope, was the first

Italian Pope in the last 30 years. He had chosen the name John 23rd in recognition of the 16th century Pope who had ruled during troubled times. It seemed appropriate for what was facing him now.

His fountain pen scratched out the names of the Cardinals he had selected on Vatican stationary: Bafile, Dulles, Dolan, Joos, Oddi, Pappalard, Foley, Daly, Gagnon, Hickey and Willebrands. Reviewing the list, he confirmed that he had a representative from every sector of the Catholic world. He signed his name, placed the Vatican seal next to it and slipped the list between pages of his Bible.

The Pope was dressed in white, as was the custom, for the day ahead. Bernard had laid out his itinerary next to his breakfast. Whispering grace, he sat down with his fruit and toasted brown bread placed with care on the small white tablecloth. Sipping his black coffee, he reviewed the time allowed for each visiting dignitary and various church groups, realizing again how little time he had left to himself.

"Good morning, Your Holiness," said Bernard.

"Good morning Bernard, I trust you had a good night's sleep?" asked the Pope.

"Yes, Your Holiness, thank you for asking."

"I have the list, Bernard. I trust that you will make confidential communication with them and will prepare for our meeting."

"Absolutely, Your Holiness, I will proceed immediately."

The folded paper with the ten names was passed to Bernard. The men that would be aware of the proposal were listed in no particular order. As it left his hand, he knew that history was beginning to play out.

Bernard returned to his small office where pictures of Jesus hung on the white washed walls next to crosses of various sizes. He felt worse than the day before. The pain in his chest was on and off again. The Vatican doctors told him he had a slight case of angina.

Sitting down, he pulled his chair closer to his wooden desk hearing its familiar creaking noise. Since the modernization of the Vatican's communication protocol, Bernard had become familiar with the Internet and its capabilities. At 68, his acceptance of this new technology was astonishing to himself and others. It was easier to do things now, especially with his arthritic hands; he didn't have to write as much anymore, just type on the keyboard, even though it was one finger typing.

Facing his computer he pressed enter to start work. The main screen stared back at him and his day began with an email to every Cardinal on the list.

The Sovereign Pontiff John 23rd requests your presence immediately at the Vatican regarding an urgent matter. Additional details of the meeting will be provided upon your arrival. His Holiness has requested that the meeting be held one week from the date listed above. I trust you will attend. Noted below are the details for travel arrangements. Accommodations will be provided at the Papal Apartments. Please notify me with your RSVP as soon as possible. I must stress that this is of utmost importance.

> *His Holiness thanks you,*
> *Yours in Christ,*
> *The Rev. Bernard Manning*

Sitting at his desk Bernard could see his cell phone vibrating, his call display showed a number that he was not familiar with. He picked up the phone and listened.

"Hello Bernard, do you know who this is?"

"I am sorry. I do not."

"Bernard, its Gordon Lynch. Remember me? My Dad was your best friend back home, remember, in

Ireland in the 60's?"

"My yes, Gordon Lynch. I haven't heard from you since you were a boy. It has been at least 30 years."

"I believe it might be a bit more, but either way it's a very long time. It's so good to hear your voice," said Gordon.

"How did you get my number? You must have gone to some trouble."

"Let's just say that I have my ways."

"Well, I should have figured that, just like your father. He could always find a way."

"You know what they say, the apple doesn't fall far from the tree," joked Gordon.

"I am sorry to hear about your father, was it about three years ago he passed away?"

"Thank you, yes, it was about three years ago. He did live a good life, hard but good, and enjoyed every minute of it. No one would say that he wasted it."

"That's for sure," Bernard replied, a hint of Irish accent creeping in with the memory, "We did have a few laughs together, actually more than a few."

"I understand that you are a big wig in the Vatican these days, Bernard, the Pope's right hand man?"

"Well I don't know if you could call me a 'big

wig'. I work for His Holiness, and I have for about ten years. Before that I worked in various positions with the Holy See. I just put a lot of time in and now I'm happy to be where I am. I have heard some rumbling about you over the years, mostly when I chatted with your Dad, he would tell me what you were up to. Last I heard you were living in the United States, New York, running some type of company, if memory serves me?"

"Yes that's right; I've had the company for going on fifteen years now. I tell you, Bernard, that has gone by fast."

"I know what you mean. The years fly by. So Gordon, what's the reason for the call, since you did say the apple doesn't fall far from the tree? I'm waiting," laughed Bernard.

"Ah, you know me too well even after all these years. But you're right, I was wondering if you could do a favour for me in memory of my father. Nothing big, but it would help me out in my business and it's just between you and me."

"Well, before I say anything, tell me what you're asking for. You know I haven't made it this far granting favors without finding out what they are first."

"I understand. I would do the same in your

position, so here is the request: I know from certain sources that there is a list being put together regarding a special meeting called by the Pope. I am creating a business proposition that will benefit the Church and may benefit others on that list. So Bernard, after saying all that, what I was wondering is if you could send me the names of the individuals so I could contact them and just let them know about it? Father would appreciate it, if he was still alive, God rest his soul. Can you do that for me?"

There was a long pause at the other end of the phone.

"Gordon, can you promise me that the business opportunity will benefit the Church and there won't be any funny stuff?"

"Bernard, I can assure you that there will be no 'funny stuff' as you put it."

"Ok then, you have my number, text me your email address and I will forward the list to you. And remember, I am doing this for your father's sake. You must keep this strictly confidential."

"Thank you Bernard, I do appreciate it, and I can assure you, when I am in Rome, we'll will have a drink together and talk about Patrick."

"I shall look forward to it. Goodbye Gordon."

"Goodbye Bernard. Thanks again."

Gordon ended the call and quickly sent a text to Bernard with his email address.

As Bernard finished sending the ten Cardinals their invitations, he began to feel warm, and his hands started to shake as they hovered above the keyboard. Sweat dripped down from his forehead and landed on his cassock. He composed an eleventh email, with nothing in the subject line, just a retyping of the names on the list and a final line that read *I trust this is what you require.*

He hit send and took a deep breath as the pain in his chest increased. He felt weak, his face grew pale and he could feel the warmth increase.

"Lord," he whispered, "Am I doing your work?"

He slumped down in his chair, still holding on to the mouse.

The noise of the ambulance siren bounced off the Vatican walls. Bernard was slumped over with one arm tangled around the arm of the chair, just as he had been found by his young administrative assistant. Vatican doctors were called to attend to him but they quickly realized that he required more care than they could provide. The medic from the ambulance administered adrenaline, trying to give his heart a needed boost.

As he was wheeled out on the stretcher towards the waiting ambulance, Bernard sensed a calmness coming over him; the bright light that everyone had spoken of had actually appeared. Lifting his hand trying to make a waving motion, he beckoned the light.

Suddenly a thud from the collapsing wheels of the gurney jarred him back to reality. He looked up to see the grey ceiling of the ambulance looking back at him. He heard the ambulance doors close tight. Then darkness fell.

Chapter 15

Cardinal Hickey was restless. Reading the invitation from the Pope was a little unnerving. He never enjoyed travelling to meetings of the College but he had gotten used to flying longer distances since becoming a Cardinal. With the right dose of drugs in his system, longer flights worked in his favour as they usually knocked him out. New York to Rome was just long enough.

His work in the boroughs of New York was his passion, now he had to make a special trip to decide on some bureaucratic crap. He replied that he would be honored to meet with Pope John, and looked forward to partaking in missions that would forward the Catholic faith. He pressed send: done. He would have to remember his vestments, which he disliked outside of mass.

Every Cardinal had responded within a day of

receiving the email, not one dared to decline such an important invitation. They arrived over the next week and were given access to the Papal apartments in the Vatican. The meeting with the Pope was set for the following Monday. They had the weekend to rest from their flights and get over jet lag, always a consideration granted to the aged. Rest was a requirement.

Cardinal Hickey traveled on Saturday, with a strong dose of Gravol in his system. With his black pants, t-shirt and a sport coat, he could almost pass for the average businessman seated in first class. The airhostess delivered the complimentary champagne and chocolates. They were gone before the last person was seated.

With everyone settled, the final announcements were made and the Airbus took off with no turbulence and on time, a rarity for LaGuardia.

The leather seat fit with room to spare for Henry. He had grown a little wider over the last ten years, and he appreciated the extra space. With the seatbelt sign now off, the service began. First class was always a treat for Henry, a rare chance to indulge himself out of the public eye.

When the hostess brought around the menu for

the flights he ordered the Beef Wellington with a glass of red wine, then looked out the oversized window at the clouds below puffed up like cotton balls.

The smell of dinner swept around the cabin and drifted into the economy section. The hostess was three seats away from delivering Henry's Beef Wellington.

"Here you are sir," she said as she placed the tray on his pull down seat tray.

"Thank you very much," Cardinal Henry replied as he eyed his meal. "Looks good. I bet it tastes good as well." He smiled up at her.

"I hope it does too sir, we don't get too many complaints." She smiled back.

Cardinal Hickey picked up his knife and fork in preparation for his dinner. He unrolled the green and red tie around the napkin and laid it on his lap. As he did, something fell out and hit the floor. The hostess, still close by, picked it up and gave it to him.

"I believe this is yours?" she said.

He took it from her, puzzled, and opened it up. It was a small piece of paper, about 4 inches by 5 inches with a hand written message. It read,

Cardinal Hickey, in advance of your visit with the Pope, I

am requesting that you contact me upon arrival in Rome. It will be of benefit to you and your congregation.

GLynch@geneqwest.com

He folded the message and put it in his jacket pocket.

I don't know any G Lynch, thought Henry, how did that get in my napkin?

"Excuse me miss," Henry said, getting the hostess's attention. "Do have any idea how this got in my napkin?"

"Sir, I can assure you that I didn't put it there. I only noticed it falling. Maybe it came out of your magazine?"

"No, I don't have a magazine. It was rolled up in the napkin, look at it, it's even curled at the ends," Henry said, showing her the rolled corners.

"I'm sorry sir, I can't help you with this. I was just assisting you with dinner." She began to look somewhat alarmed and Henry realized that he should stop questioning her before things escalated.

"Yes, I understand, I apologize for the questions. It's just strange. How would someone know that I was going to get that particular knife and fork set?"

"Maybe a sign from above?" joked the hostess, unaware of the irony of her statement.

"Maybe you're right about that."

Looking around the seating area in first class, Henry's suspicions grew as he stared at each passenger. Trying to identify traits or hints that would give the culprit away, he inspected every detail of each person. Someone around him was watching him; someone knew where he was headed.

The wheels of the Airbus touched down, reverse thrusters came to life and Air Italia flight 684 came to a stop. The usual announcements could be heard in three languages. The clack of released seatbelts sounded like applause.

Henry stared out of his window, watching as a flurry of ground crew surround the plane like worker bees attending to the queen. He turned on his Blackberry to check his emails. Thirty-two emails from various church functionaries. Things to attend to, things to ignore. He pulled the folded message out of his jacket pocket, reread it, and wondered whether to reply. His mind was racing with questions and curiosity. *How did he know I was meeting the Pope? How did he know what flight I was on? How did he know I was even invited?*

He gathered his things from the seat pocket in front of him and stood up to exit the plane. He stretched his body in preparation for walking. As he got older, longer flights were taking a toll on his body; it was one of the reasons he hated flying.

The door of the plane opened and the First Class passengers filed out. The flight attendants, using one of three languages, thanked every passenger.

Waiting for his luggage Henry looked at his Blackberry again, wondering whether to email this mystery man. He pulled up the compose message screen and typed in GLynch@geneqwest.com.

Mr. GLynch, I am not sure how you know me.

He pressed send, put the phone back in his holster and waited for his luggage. Pulling his one piece of luggage off the carousel, he wheeled it toward the customs area. The mingling of hundreds of people sent a constant hum through the room. He stood in line waiting his turn. Looking into space, trying to kill time, he glanced at the various color photos of Rome on the wall. The Coliseum, the Vatican and the Italian countryside invited tourists to enjoy the finer things of Italy.

He noticed Cardinal Gustaff Joos in line. He was

from South Africa, and they had kept in contact because of a friendship that formed at the last two meetings of Cardinals. They had found that they were both practical men with clear goals and ambitions. Henry waved in the direction of Gustaff, hoping to catch his attention. Gustaff saw an arm waving, and gave a smaller wave of acknowledgement. After clearing customs they chatted outside the terminal about the upcoming meeting, to discover that both of them were unaware of its nature or duration.

"Are you heading there now?" asked Gustaff.

"I think I'll take a little detour before I get entrenched in the Vatican," smiled Henry.

"Ok Henry, so I will see you later," Gustaff stepped into a waiting car.

"Yes, I won't be much later, just want to get some of that Italian flavor before I get behind locked doors."

Gustaff closed the car door and smiled, sending a goodbye wave in the direction of Henry. The car pulled away from the curb heading in the direction of the Vatican.

Henry stood at the edge of the curb and hailed a cab. It had been a few years since his last visit to Rome and he wanted to see the Coliseum again. Henry watched from the back seat as the cab weaved in and out of traffic, dodging pedestrians and taking chances. *Not much different than driving in New York,* Henry thought.

He felt the vibration of his Blackberry on his hip. He had turned off the ringer at LaGuardia and forgotten to reset it. Pulling it from his holster he looked at the screen. Email from GLynch. He looked at the passing scenery, wondering whether to take this any further. He continued to look out at the window waiting for the Coliseum to come into view.

"Here you are sir, that will 65 Euros please."

Reaching into his pocket he pulled out his money, thumbed through the colorful bills, gave the cab driver 75 Euros and closed the car door. He looked up at the stone walls that history had left standing.

He pulled out his Blackberry again, opening his email. GLynch was still there.

Cardinal Hickey, I have a representative close by, would you be prepared to meet? I have a proposition for you that will benefit yourself and your congregation.

Is there more to it than that? Henry emailed back.

No.

Ok, let me know when and where, I have to be at the Vatican in 2 hours.

Our representative will contact you in 10 minutes.

Standing on the sidewalk in front of the Coliseum, Henry looked around searching for the contact. Everyone was a possibility.

Suddenly a sizeable hand rested on his shoulder. Henry immediately felt heat emanate through his shirt

"Cardinal Hickey, my name is John Abbott. Thank you for meeting with me. Would you like to have a coffee?" he said all in one breath, pointing in the direction of the nearest cafe.

Turning around Henry glanced up at a large man with salt and pepper hair dressed in casual summer pants and a linen shirt.

"Certainly my son. Maybe on the way you can tell me what this is all about. I have a lot of questions concerning an unusual item I found at lunch on the plane. Do you know anything about that?" Henry said falling back into his clerical demeanor.

Sitting at a small circular table outside of the café, John began to outline the purpose of the meeting. All of Henry's questions were answered and in an hour Henry had grasped the gravity of the situation in full.

"Henry, before I leave I just have one other thing I would like to present to you." John pulled a sealed white envelope from his jacket pocket. He slid it across the table stopping just short of Henry's crossed hands. "Inside is a proposal to you that we would like you to consider. I would prefer you don't open it here, but when you have had a chance to review it, please let us know if you can help us."

Henry stared at John, eyebrows raised inquisitively. He took the envelope and put it in his pants pocket.

"Henry, we are both businessmen of sorts. Sometimes in business deals are struck that the public never needs or gets to know. This may be one of those times."

Getting up from the table John motioned to his watch, "Have to go Henry, let me know what you think of our proposal. Talk to you soon." He reached out to shake hands.

"Ok, John, goodbye." Henry watched John thread through the tables with ease and reached the street.

Sitting alone in the café Henry reached for the envelope, glanced around for onlookers and opened it. Pulling out the folded single page of humid feeling paper, he began to read.

Cardinal Hickey, thank you for opening this letter. We trust that after you read the text below you will destroy it.

Shortly you will be faced with a daunting task. You will be asked to decide on how to move the world and the Catholic religion forward. We have a proposal of great benefit to both of us. We would ask you to influence the decision, to sway the verdict in favour of acceptance by whatever means you deem appropriate. If you agree to this we will deposit **five million US dollars** *into a Swiss bank account by the end of decision day. You will never see us or hear from us again. Contact us by phone or text at the noted number. Imagine the good you will be able to accomplish.*

Thank you.

John Abbott

Chapter 16

At the Vatican, Monsignor Domus took the place of the ailing Bernard to greet the arriving Cardinals. He welcomed them one by one and gave them the itinerary for the next two days that Bernard had prepared in advance. It contained the private chamber numbers for each Cardinal, meeting times and room locations.

The first task was a breakfast meeting with the Pope the following morning at 9a.m., in the Courtyard of Sixtus. The three storey tan brick building was lined with rows of columns and a statue of the Virgin Mary was perched high on one wall overlooking St Peter's Square. She had been keeping watch there since the 17th century.

Last time Henry had stayed at the Vatican the apartments were in disrepair with leaky pipes and terrible lighting. They had been left to decline and were severely out of date. He was pleasantly surprised when he turned the key to open the locked door to his room. It had been updated and was much more comfortable. The warm lights, white curtains with blue sashes and restored marble floors made a big difference. Some designer has had a hand in this, Henry thought.

He noted the clean smell as he entered and the seal of the Vatican that was emblazoned on the tightly fitted white sheets and bedspread. Removing his scuffed running shoes he placed them carefully in the corner next to the only table in the room. The white room was equipped with everything he needed. A large wooden crucifix of Jesus on the cross was prominently displayed on the wall over the bed.

The doorless bathroom in the far corner of the room consisted of a small shower, white toilet and basin with hanging crested white hand towels neatly folded over the bar. Soaps and toothbrush were provided. No toothpaste. Still, it was much improved since his last visit.

Henry closed the door and sat on the bed, removed his socks and curled up for a nap.

The sun shone through the lone window, waking Henry up. It was six a.m. and he had three hours before the first meeting. Showered and shaved, he headed over to the Cortile Della Pigna. The sun-steeped ten-minute walk warmed up his aching body.

The nine other Cardinals were already there. The guests mingled awkwardly. Some knew each other; many were looking to meet their counterparts.

Henry recognized two friends immediately. Elevated to Cardinal after years of service, Cardinal Gustaff Joos had garnered media attention in past years as an outspoken advocate for changes to in the Catholic Church. Never content with the status quo, he was always looking for ways to engage people into the fold. At 60, his friendship with Pope John had been rewarded on numerous occasions, usually to the benefit of his diocese. Not one to mince his words, his South African upbringing had provided him the opportunity to witness great injustices and he was vocal about apartheid and its effects on his country. His piercing blue eyes and engaging smile combined with his eloquent delivery often disarmed his critics and provided a platform for his radical opinions. He gave voice to opinions that the Pope could not speak aloud.

Off to one side of the group, 70-year old Cardinal John Foley mingled with two others in the group. Conservative in his opinions, he had once written a letter to the Pope in favour of retaining the Latin mass. He still read the mass in Latin for a few holdouts in his congregation. Raised in Boston by a family that was well connected politically and had influenced business leaders in the community, his voice was powerful and respected.

"Good morning to all of you, I trust you are rested. I welcome all of you to the Vatican. I know each of you have been here before in various capacities." As he spoke the Monsignor spread his arms, seemingly gathering up the entire group in a friendly embrace.

"So please, make the most of the beautiful day and breakfast will be served outside shortly. Gentlemen, I hope you enjoy your time here with His Holiness." The Monsignor pointed to the serving tent where table and chairs had been set up, motioning the group to head in that direction.

The morning sun at their backs and a slight breeze created a perfect setting for breakfast al fresco. They each took a white china plate set with the Vatican emblem and paraded along the white cloth covered table sampling fruits, breads and eggs. As they took their places at two round tables with their coffee or tea, the same question was on everyone's mind.

"So what is this about?" Henry asked. "Does

anyone know?

Ancient grey stone walls framed the formal garden where the group had gathered around one table. Some were finishing their last coffee, and others were taking in the beauty and order of the intricate gravel pathways and fragrant arrangements of flowers.

They now had the opportunity to get to know each other a little better and talk about common issues. The discussions circled back to the nature of the meeting called by the Pope but the questions remained unanswered. The more patient Cardinals enjoyed a quiet moment in the warm sun.

From one quadrant of the garden the large wooden door strained to open on its massive black hinges. With a push, it began to move in the direction of the group. Once it swung free, four Swiss Guards marched through in unison, entering the courtyard. Their slow pace matched that of the Pope. He was contained in the middle of a moving box of guards. They followed the gravel pathway and at the intersection of the pathways they turned right towards the Cardinals. The Pope was looking straight ahead. The Cardinals stopped their conversation and turned to the box of men. Some whispered to each other, keeping their conversation to a minimum. The Swiss Guards reached the breakfast area, turned in toward each other and stood at attention. The Pope emerged from between them to join the waiting group.

He walked slowly toward the Cardinals raising his hand to greet them; a sense of peace seemed to emanate from him. He smiled at the group and his eyes rested upon each of them in turn. He appeared somewhat tired as he made the sign of the cross over them.

"Good morning all, I trust you have enjoyed a nourishing breakfast on this beautiful morning."

Affirmations and greetings rang out from the group.

"I want to thank you all for coming here on such short notice. I know you are all doing important work for your parishioners and churches. It is with a heavy heart I call you here. I have some important matters to discuss with you and I am sure by now you realize that you are a select group. I have chosen you because of your experience, your wisdom and your dedication to our faith. I will be calling on you to assist me in some decisions that will affect more than just this group. In fact it will affect..." He paused. "I will discuss these matters today when we meet. You will each be notified with the particulars.   Please my friends, take pleasure in the morning, we will convene in the Segnatura Room at ten o'clock."

The Pope's words were measured. His breathing was shallow as he returned to the Swiss Guard's protection.   The box formed around the Pope and he returned the same way he had entered and with a small wave of his hand he was gone. The Cardinals waited until the wooden door closed before they started to discuss the situation.

A few took guesses as to the reasoning behind the selection of the ten cardinals.   Some wondered if demands for the Vatican to make some changes to its principles or dogma was the key issue. Others in the group believed there might be pressure to allow women to become priests. Issues like these were pushing the Church to modernize and accommodate younger congregations.

"Whatever it is, my brothers, this sounds like it will be a long couple of days and nights," said Cardinal Daly.

"Why would he just select ten of us? I know he said that it was because of our dedication, but all the Cardinals have the same dedication.   Do we have something in common that we don't know about?" said Cardinal Dulles jokingly.

Two hours later the group of ten arrived at the meeting room.

The tall, engraved double doors with their brass plates and sturdy handles stood in front of them like soldiers on guard. Cardinal Bafile was the first to enter. The large oval desk surrounded by eleven black leather chairs sat proudly in the middle of the room, its carved paw feet planted firmly on the dark oak floor. A large chandelier hung overhead. The Pope had arrived through a private entrance and was standing at the far end of the room waiting for them. Facing the group as they entered, he opened his arms to greet them.

"Good morning," he said, moving to the head of the table.

In front of each chair was a document with a blank cover - Gordon Lynch's proposal.

"Before we start, let us pray together for God's guidance. Please bow your heads in prayer with me."

Standing behind their chairs they bowed their heads and waited for the blessing.

"Heavenly Father, you have tasked us with a most

difficult decision. We pray for your guidance in this matter. We understand that you have given us this task to lead our followers towards your promise of life everlasting. Please make us strong and show us the way."

They lifted their heads, followed the Pope's lead and sat down.

The Pope raised the document up from the desk in his aged hands, gripping it tightly, almost angrily.

"Eminences, in front of you is a document that was sent to me via our New York representative from a person unknown to our community. What you have in front of you has been seen only by me. Please take a few minutes and read its contents. I believe that once you have finished you will understand why I have called you to this summit. You will understand the sensitivity of the situation and will further understand why it must remain within this room. Please begin." He motioned to them to open the document.

One by one the Cardinals turned to the first page. It began with the words:

We would like to introduce you to GeneQwest and our latest discovery.

In our research labs in Bristol, England, our team has

been working with the latest technology and the best researchers in the world. Over the last six months some astounding results have come to our attention with an unparalled discovery in Montana in the United States by two paleontologists of an unfossilized skin sample from a T-Rex and its infant.

This unique sample provided the opportunity for our team to perform DNA tests in search of the chemical makeup of these magnificent creatures. It provided us with a window to view life as it existed over sixty five million years ago. It was an amazing opportunity for our company, GeneQwest, to learn secrets that had been considered lost forever. Our team dedicated itself to testing theories and hypotheses from the paleontological world to find possible benefits for the pharmaceutical division of our company. It was our goal to discover the keys to DNA development that would benefit people in the world today. It was our mandate to put our discovery to use in the most effective way for all of humanity.

You are the first to see our results. We have not, nor do we ever intend to publish to the general media. This information will not appear in scientific publications and we have taken the most stringent of security measures to protect our intellectual property.

The following eight pages are a summary of our results and conclusions. All the information that follows has been collected by our lead researcher; he is the only one that knows the final implications and conclusions. He has compiled the results based on *industry accepted test methodology.*

The following pages were crammed with graphs, test methods and results that were not understood by most of the Cardinals. The Pope glanced through the document while he waited for them to finish. He got up and paced around the room, occasionally checking as he passed each Cardinal to see where they were in the document.

They continued with their reading.

The preceding information illustrates our methods of scientific measurement and verified conclusions. How does this impact the Roman Catholic faith? How can it help you with your mission to lead people to your faith?

The results of our work are so significant that GeneQwest is willing to share an opportunity that will be of immense value to you.

In summary, we have discovered the reason for the extinction of the dinosaurs. We have unlocked their DNA through this skin sample to reveal the answer to their disappearance. It appears that there was a latent gene that began to mutate at precisely the time of their extinction. This latent gene was a time bomb for the entire species. We discovered that it started with smaller species, until it reached the dinosaurs of enormous size. Eventually all of them died out. It was a physiologically determined extinction

How does this affect the Roman Catholic Church? How does what happened sixty-five million years ago affect us today and in particular, your congregations?

Our research shows that this gene is active at the present moment. We have tested various mammals and discovered the same pattern. We have been able to identify this latent gene. Most exciting of all is the fact that we have been able to control its effects and stop the extinction of any identified target species. Why is this important?

We have identified the same gene in humans. We have seen the results, tested the hypothesis and we predict that it will have the same effect on all humans within a one to five year period. The same gene that eliminated the dinosaurs has begun to mutate in human beings. We are next.

Most the Cardinals reached this statement around the same time. There was a moment of astonishment as one by one they paused and looked up at the others. The Pope knew they had reached the first revelation and turned away, waiting for their reaction to what was to come.

We are prepared to offer you a solution to the problem. GeneQwest would like to partner with the Church to offer you the exclusive opportunity to save the mortal lives of your followers and to provide new members of the Church with the same cure. We will provide you with the means to give every Catholic the chance to live on Earth and in Heaven and to be the destined survivors of this mass extinction. It will give you the chance to demonstrate that God has selected the one true faith. Beyond life everlasting after death, the Church will become the only option for survival on Earth. It will benefit humanity and you will become the most powerful religion the world has ever known.

We are prepared to offer you our research findings for three billion US dollars. The appendix at the end of this proposal will demonstrate how we propose to provide your followers with the serum needed to stop the gene's progress.

GeneQwest thanks you in advance for your consideration.

Cardinal Foley was the last to finish reading. He closed the proposal and folded his hands in prayer, head tilted upwards. The other Cardinals sat silently, stunned at what they had just read. Some tapped their pens against their hands; others opened the proposal and pretended to read it again. The atmosphere in the room felt thick with anxiety. They all understood the choice in front of them.

The Pope returned to his position at the head of the table. Still standing, he rubbed his forehead, feeling the beads of sweat on his fingers.

"My sons, you can now understand why I have called you together. It was my feeling that I alone could not make such a decision. I need your trusted advice for this situation. As you can see from the proposal, we have a dilemma to contend with. We have a situation so grave and so important that what we decide will affect billions of people. We need to discuss, decide and implement the means to handle this. Now more than ever we will need the power of God to help us make the right decision."

After his speech the Pope sat back down in his chair, his arms folded around his body. He leaned forward and opened his copy of the proposal.

"I want to start with a few words about what we have done in advance of this meeting. I want to give you an understanding of our efforts and results," he said, turning to another document he had placed next to the proposal.

"Here in this document is a summary of The Pontifical Academy of Science's research and investigation of GeneQwest and its past work. It provided us with the opportunity to disprove or discredit GeneQwest. We have gone down every avenue to do this. There is nothing. Their claim of what they have discovered is correct. I will pass around their conclusions. It appears that we have to decide on a course of action based on this information. I trust you will help me and please speak freely. Let me open by asking Cardinal Foley for his opinion."

The Cardinal stood up and straightened his shoulders and spoke out commandingly in his broad Boston accent. "Throughout our history it has always been our role as Cardinals to guide our Bishops and the faithful. We have all acted out of a spiritual perspective; we respect the foundations of Catholicism. Since I finished this document," he said, raising it in the air, "I fear for those foundations. I have never seen or read anything that will affect the church around the world as much as this. It seems to me that we have no choice but to deny this offer and trust in the will of God. After all, if He has decided that we have served Him in this world to our best capabilities, then He has other plans for us. Therefore, I believe that we must step aside and let His guidance rule. How can we question the decisions of God? It is not our place to do such a thing."

He sat back down in his chair, looking around for input or comment on his opinion.

"Thank you, Cardinal Foley, I appreciate your wisdom and your thoughts. It is my intention to get everyone sitting around this table to speak their mind. You must be true to yourself, I must hear from each and every one of you. Remember, our faith is strong. Our faith is what will lead our decisions. Please, can I ask Cardinal Willebrands to come forth with his thoughts?"

The Pope waved his hand in the direction of Johannes, inviting him to stand.

Cardinal Willebrands got up from his chair, and nodded his acceptance of the Pope's request. "Thank you, Your Holiness. I appreciate you asking all of us around this table to have input into this most difficult decision. I'm afraid I must disagree with Cardinal Foley. I understand his passion and commitment to our faith, but I believe we can look at this as an opportunity to lead the world. If God is in our thoughts, then He has given me another point of view from Cardinal Foley. We must ask ourselves 'why'?

"Do we know the right thing to do? How do we persuade each other of our opinions? For me, Your Holiness, it comes down to one thing. God will influence us to find the choice that will benefit the Church and the people of the world. I believe that we must continue on with our work. We must increase our followers, as we know that it will lead them to salvation. It will lead them to the Word of the Lord; there is no other religion that can provide them with it. If we, as Catholics, ignore the opportunity to guide others to the Lord we are ignoring our responsibility to God and His people. I feel that we must engage the offer from GeneQwest and move forward as quickly as possible." He returned to his chair, glad that he had given his opinion and interested in the discussion to come.

"Well thank you Cardinal Willebrands. We now have two different directions to consider, I would now like to hear from Cardinal Hickey," the Pope requested.

"First, like the others," Henry began, "I thank Your Holiness for including me in this select group. It is truly an honor to be seated among men of such reverence and faith. I feel blessed. To address the question at hand I would ask you consider how we came to be sitting in this room dealing with this issue. It strikes me that from our beginnings as priests we've seen ourselves as servants of the Lord. Our interpretation of the messages our Lord sends us may differ, our personalities may differ, but the thread of consistency through all of these is our faith, our guiding light. It is with that in mind that I feel we must make sure - it must become our mandate - that we let others into this great gathering we call Catholicism. If we accept the offer from GeneQwest it may appear that we are going against the word of God. But I believe we should accept the offer from GeneQwest and watch our followers grow in numbers and in faith because of their belief in the one true God, which we all believe works through each and every one of us, even Mr. Gordon Lynch. Thank you."

Taking his seat at the table, Henry felt confident that he had summed up his point of view so that few could argue it. His face was ruddy from the exertion and he could feel his heartbeat slowly returning to normal.

"Thank you Cardinal Hickey for those words, we will continue around the table," said the Pope.

For the next three hours they were locked in discussions that threatened to become arguments. At times the process was difficult and uncomfortable.

It became obvious there were two camps, two well-defined positions. Many Cardinals steadfastly refused. Even those considering the proposal had questions. They wondered about the consequences if it was discovered that that they had deceived their followers. How did you stop information from leaking out to the masses? How would they get the serum to their parishioners, and what was to happen to the church if they didn't do anything, and worst of all, if the cure fell into the hands of other faiths?

Finally, Pope John declared the afternoon's session over. He was tired and he could see that they had reached a philosophical stalemate. He pressed the button to control the guarded doors and they swung open, bringing a refreshing breeze in from the hallway.

"We will break for dinner and resume shortly after," said the Pope as they exited.

Leaving the boardroom the Cardinals headed for the courtyard where they had had their breakfast. The morning sun had given way to the evening's thick humid air. In informal groups of three or four the Cardinals huddled, discussing what they had read.

"Can you believe it all?" Cardinal Joos asked. "I can't even fathom the consequences."

"I agree, it seems to me like blackmail," Cardinal Foley added. "How are we expected to make the right decision? Is there a right decision?"

"Depends on how we run our business I guess," interjected Cardinal Hickey. "Either way, what we decide will have costs. It just depends who we decide to put them on."

The conversation made its way around the group, rising and falling in volume and pitch as they talked. Their voices grew quieter around the hour that they were to reconvene. Eventually Cardinal Bafile motioned to the group that they should head back.

Returning to the meeting room, they took the same seats as before. Cardinal Hickey and Cardinal Willebrands sat next to each other. The ten Cardinals sat silently in anticipation of the final decision required at the end of the day.

At the head of the table sat the Pope in his white cassock with a pectoral cross suspended by a gold chain resting on his chest. With his hands folded in front of him he made a triangle with his two index fingers, creating a steeple. He waited patiently for all his Cardinals to be settled around the large table.

"Once again," he began, "we are gathered together to continue our discussion. There have been many times that I have been required to make a decision knowing it will affect the life of our Church. This decision, being the most important in our history, has left me with the same feeling of responsibility. We must listen to God speaking through us. We must listen to His word coming into our thoughts. He has always guided me with His loving hand to where I should be and need to be. He knows what we should do, He knows what will be best for all, but in our earthly world we must search out His word. We must follow it. I believe He has touched you all in some way. Listen to those words.

"So let's begin with a short summary of what has been presented to us. Earlier we had a few people express their opinions. I would like to encourage the others who did not have a chance to let their views be known.

He quickly referred to the notes to see who had not spoken. "Cardinal Gagnon, I believe you have not had a chance to speak. Please can we have your views on the subject?"

The Cardinal nodded assent. He went over the different views already tabled and then talked about what he felt was important to himself and the church. He was an eloquent speaker, engaging his audience from beginning to end. His conclusion: he was not in favour of accepting the offer from GeneQwest.

The Pope went around the table soliciting the Cardinals' opinions and their views on the impact to their respective areas of the world. It was two hours before there was a break for them to use the facilities and stretch their ageing legs. It was clear that the pontiff expected everyone back in the room quickly and that the goal today was to come to a consensus on how to approach this delicate decision. As the Cardinals exited the room the Pope checked his white cell phone and scrolled through the lines of emails.

The subject line of one email caught his eye. *Decision?* He opened it to find no text in the body of the email.

The Pope felt a rush of blood to his face. His hands went clammy and his lips unconsciously pinched together. How did Gordon Lynch get his secured email address? He wished this was not happening. Moving gingerly, he left the room, looking for a chair. He found a bench left behind by some workers who were repairing the ceiling. As he sat down on the foldable metal bench it marked his white cassock with a grey metal line. He deleted the email and put the phone in his pocket under his robe. He made the steeple again with his index fingers but this time it was accompanied with a prayer whispered under his breath and a look upwards.

He returned to the boardroom shaken and determined to take action.

Standing among the Cardinals, still disturbed by the email, the Pontiff walked around the room deep in thought before sitting down. He frowned with concern.

"I would like to continue our debate, but I must implore you to be concise with your points of view. I believe by the end of the evening we must reach a decision along with a strategy on moving forward.

"Cardinal Joos, please commence," the Pope said, pointing in his direction.

"Thank you Holy Father," Cardinal Joos said with a heavy accent, "I would like to begin with a story."

The other Cardinals sat back in anticipation of a lengthy diatribe.

"When I first started as a junior priest, I witnessed some compelling life stories from parishioners. They varied from deaths in their families to physical abuse. Now, as a Cardinal and an older priest, I continue to listen to my flock. One consistent theme throughout all I have heard is that they had turned to God for answers. It has helped many get through extremely difficult times. My question to you - to us - is whether we are prepared to take that away from people? Can you imagine the effect on the masses if it was shown that we were part of a scheme that was focused on increasing numbers instead of working the love of God? I implore you not to accept this offer. It could lead to the reverse of what is being proposed; it could lead to an exodus of followers if any of this was leaked or discovered. Please make the right decision and tell Mr. Gordon Lynch we decline his offer."

"Thank you Cardinal Joos, we will conclude with Cardinal Pappalard. Please, Cardinal, let us know your feelings on this matter."

"Thank you Your Excellency, I will keep my view short in the interest of time. I believe after hearing everyone's opinions that we must accept the offer. We must truly believe that our Lord is guiding us and that he has put Mr. Lynch in front of us as a test - a test of our faith, a test of our dedication to His word. In Corithians it states, 'So that your faith might not rest in the wisdom of men, but in the power of God.' We must not deny him. The Bible tells us that those who disobey will feel his wrath. In conclusion, I would implore us to take the offer in the understanding that it is not GeneQwest offering this up to us, but God himself. Thank you." Cardinal Pappalard looked over at the Pope to indicate that he had finished.

The group had reached the end of their capabilities; the outcome of their opinions and conclusions hovered in the room like an impending rain cloud.

The Pope stood up. "Thank you for all your words, I know they come from your loving hearts. It is a difficult decision we all face, and it is a troubled time for us and our faith. The decision in front of us is not one I believed I would ever have to make. We do not have any precedent to guide us. I must tell you that I am not at peace with myself about what we have to do. I am seeking help from you and from Him who has been with us throughout this day. I must ask you to pray with me and ask Him for direction. Please, let us bow our heads and ask for His guidance and love. If there ever was a time in our history for Him to assist us it is now."

They all bowed their heads, listening to the Pope's short prayer.

"Beloved Father, provide us with Your heavenly guidance. We are in Your care, we are in Your hands, please help us with the decision that we face. Amen."

The room was silent. Then the Pope raised his head and spoke of procedures.

"As is required, we will vote and move forward with the majority. We will continue until we have a verdict. Please contemplate your decision and place your vote in the box in the adjacent room."

They were all familiar with the procedure. The selection of each Pope was done in the same way. The only difference would be that there would be no smoke rising from the Vatican this time.

One by one the Cardinals made their way to the next room. The small room was often used by dignitaries who had requested a private discussion with the Pope. Two green upholstered armchairs sat in the middle of the room where matching curtains hung from ceiling to floor. A ballot box with a slit in the top sat on a small desk situated directly opposite the door.

Each Cardinal entered separately with a folded ballot in hand to place inside the box. The ten Cardinals quickly completed the task and returned to the boardroom. After the last Cardinal had entered the Pope picked up the box from the other room and returned with it to reveal the verdict.

It had been seven hours since they started. They were weary, but their interest in the verdict kept them on edge. The Pope opened the box and began to pull out their papers one by one.

As the evening had progressed the Pope's posture had slowly deteriorated. Hunched over the ballot box, he reached in and pulled out the remaining votes. His hands had a tiny shake to them, a nervous twitch that fired simultaneously on both hands. The Cardinals noticed the shake was getting worse. He unfolded the last two papers and pressed them flat on the table in front of him. All ten were displayed on the veneered table, each turned upside down. He began to turn them over slowly one by one.

The first to be turned over was a 'No'. He looked up, with a slight smile pulling up the corner of his mouth. The next one was also a 'No'. He continued turning over the papers, putting the 'No' votes on one side and 'Yes' votes on the other side of the box. The sixth vote created a tie, the seventh and eight indicated a nudge to acceptance of the offer; it was now five to three in favour of taking the offer from GeneQwest.

The Pope's trust began to fade. Had he selected the right Cardinals for this task? Could he rely on their decision? He picked up the last two votes, flattening them, lining them up precisely with the others. He turned them over slowly; all eyes around the table were straining to see the last two.

As both were revealed, it showed the count to be six to four in favour of accepting the offer. Stunned silence fell over the table. Someone had changed their mind between the discussion and the vote. No one knew who had switched. No one knew why.

"It has become apparent that the group is in favour of accepting the GeneQwest proposal," said the Pope.

"I know you have asked God for His help and the Holy Spirit has reached each of you. I have asked for the same help and guidance. I will be taking this verdict under consideration, as I have to make preparations in addressing how we move forward. I thank you again and request that we retire for the night. We will meet again tomorrow morning at eight and I will brief you on our future plans. God Bless you and good night."

The Pope made the sign of the cross and waited for them all to exit before he got up. He picked up the ballots and stacked them on top of each other creating a small pile which he folded and put in his pocket under his cassock.

He was aware of the scratching sound his feet made as they dragged across the stone floor. Exhausted by the day's events he returned to his private quarters where he slowly lowered himself on to his bed. Kicking off his shoes, he looked up in search of an answer. None came.

Darkness soon stole his thoughts and replaced them with sleep.

Chapter 17

A small box with Bernard's belongings was gathered together by the Vatican staff. The intention was to provide Bernard with familiar items to aid in his recovery. Its contents included his beloved white ivory cross from above his bed, his reading glasses and the journal from his night table and his well-rubbed rosary beads. All rested neatly in the velvet-lined box accompanied by his medication. A small piece of wheeled luggage would transport a few clothes for his undetermined length of stay at the Vatican hospital.

Closing the lid, Monsignor Domus carried the box to the Pope's quarters.

"Your Holiness, here is the box going over to Bernard. You requested it to be delivered to you once we had completed the task."

"Yes, thank you, just place it on the table," he said, pointing to the empty surface near the window.

"Will there be anything else Your Holiness?"

"No, thank you, that will be all."

Bowing, Domus turned and left the room, closing the door behind him.

Standing over the box, note in hand, Pope John reviewed his words one final time.

My dear friend Bernard,

In this troubling time, my hope is that you will return in good health. You and I have had a long journey together and your advice and friendship has always been meaningful to me. I pray for your safe return and I know God will work in His way to see you and I together again soon.

John

He looked into the open box, wondering where to place his words of encouragement and, without thinking, he picked up what he knew was Bernard's journal. Holding the journal in his hand, the Pope flicked through the pages, stopping at the last written page to place his folded note.

Undersized crooked black inked letters ran the length of the page. As he wrestled with the desire to read the last entry he noticed two words emerging from the cryptic scribbling: *Gordon Lynch.* He continued to read.

October 10th

Helping Gordon Lynch further the Catholic faith, list of Cardinals sent via email. Look forward to seeing the results of efforts and seeing Gordon again.

He realized his friend and trusted employee had been deceived into thinking he was helping the faith, when in fact Bernard had set in motion a scenario that could end in a Vatican scandal.

The Pope now understood how Gordon had got his email, and wondered how much Gordon had infiltrated the inner sanctum under the guise of benefiting the Church.

Bernard's hospitalization lasted a week. When he arrived the doctors in attendance diagnosed a mild heart attack and it was later confirmed to be stress related. Bernard was ordered to rest and stay away from any issues that might incite a relapse. He was well looked after by the staff; his grandfatherly demeanor made him a favorite of the nurses who fussed over him at every opportunity. Vatican staff came to visit with words of encouragement and the Pope had scheduled an early morning visit for the next day.

"Good morning Bernard. I trust you are getting better each day?" asked the Pope.

Still slightly groggy from medication, Bernard's weary eyes looked up and he answered, "Yes, thank you, Your Holiness. I believe I am moving in the right direction."

"That is good, Bernard. I am praying for you at every mass."

"Thank you."

"If you are able, may I ask you a question?"

"Certainly, Your Grace."

"It is about your association with Gordon Lynch."

Bernard could sense his skin changing colour; he assumed his cheeks were glowing in acknowledgement. "I have known Gordon since he was a young boy."

"I am sure you have, but there are things he is trying to do that will have some serious effects on you, me, and the rest of the Church."

Looking anxious Bernard tried to reposition himself on the bed, preparing himself for the Pope's words.

"Bernard, I know that you have sent him the names of several of our Cardinals, and I believe that you acted from a place of trust, but is there anything else I should know about this man?"

"Your Grace, I am truly sorry if I have erred in judgment. My intentions were and will always rest with our Church. I trusted Gordon with information on the belief that he was doing good. He had promised me that he would serve our faith, but I assume from your words that he has not honoured his pledge. I suspect I have been deceived by him," said Bernard looking up in resignation.

"Bernard," the Pope reached out to hold his trembling hand, "You have always been a trusted servant of the Lord. Now is not the time to doubt your decisions. Gordon will have his day in front of God. Do you know of anyone else that he might be in communication with?"

Looking up at the Pope, Bernard motioned to the Pope to come closer, his voice a whisper.

"I believe there is another aiding his efforts, but I do not know who. Please, Your Grace, forgive me for my actions, I cannot believe I did what I did."

"Rest, my son, time is needed for you to heal.

You are not in need of forgiveness; you are in need of God's peace."

Bernard's grip weakened and the Pope stayed until he felt the warm sensation of Bernard's hand leave his grasp. He placed Bernard's worn cross and rosary beads between his folded arms, made the sign of the cross and said goodbye to his friend.

He left the room walking slowly down the dimly lit hallway. He passed the attending nurse and continued to the exit in silent prayer.

When he heard of Bernard's death the next day, he was glad that he had stayed a few moments longer.

The condolences came in from everyone that knew Bernard. The announcement of his death stressed his years of loyalty and dedication to the Vatican. A personal note from the Pope expressed how much he would miss Bernard and how he knew God would welcome him with open arms.

Chapter 18

Every day began with mass and a prayer for the counsel and heavenly wisdom that directed his path.

The stained glass ceiling in the Pope's private chapel splashed sunlight on the marble floor, bouncing blues and greens onto the walls. A small covered table with six glowing candles sat at the front of the room. The curved back wall wrapped around Jesus on the cross.

Earlier the Pope had served mass to the few invitees who were honored to receive the Eucharist from His Holiness. Now alone, the Pope slumped in silence in a low backed chair in the centre of the room. Statues of former Popes stood on their pedestals lining both walls above his head, guarding the faith. Resting his elbow on the arm of the chair, he leaned in, placing his head into his hands. In the quietness of the chapel he communed with God.

Mindful of his purpose, he reflected on his past

and his journey. He thought of his parents, devout followers of the faith who were thankful that their prayers for their only son had been answered. After three miscarriages, they believed their son was a gift from God. They thought he would be destined for a life with the Lord.

Giving himself a brief respite from the problem at hand, Lorenzo Corsini reminisced about his life before the priesthood, before becoming Pope. Working with his father at a local haberdashery in Naples, he learned the craft of suit making and learned from his father that there were many different ways to take the measure of a man. He thought of his adoring mother and her unwavering faith. She had asked him to listen for the calling and when it came, she guided him into the seminary. Lorenzo never hesitated; he fully embraced the journey and he recalled his mother's smile when he graduated from the seminary. She knew God was working through her son.

He wondered if he was doing God's work now.

Chapter 19

February 26th

A delicate knock on the door of the Pope's room echoed in the hallway as Monsignor Domus waited to enter. He carried a tray of coffee, toasted pumpernickel bread and plain yoghurt.

The door opened and Marcel Domus saw a tired and aged man, disheveled and not completely dressed. It seemed that he had fallen asleep with his clothes on. The Pope motioned for Marcel to enter the room.

"Your Holiness, I took the privilege of bringing you some breakfast. I thought you might be in need of some added privacy after last night."

"Thank you Marcel, that was very kind," said the Pope, turning to him with a smile.

Marcel placed the tray on the table and looked to see if he was required further. He waited but there was no answer. He left without a sound and slowly closed the door.

While finishing breakfast, the Pope prepared himself for the final meeting with his Cardinals. Leaving his quarters a half hour early, he walked slowly, thinking over his decision.

When he pushed the door open, the Cardinals had just finished breakfast and were waiting for him.

"Good morning," said the Pope, seating himself at the head of the table.

"Good morning, Your Holiness," the group replied as one.

"I will get right to the point. Last night the vote revealed the direction preferred by the group. The majority believed we should accept the offer from GeneQwest. I respect your verdict, but I cannot accept it."

The sudden announcement caught the group off guard. They sat as silent as mannequins in a storefront.

"I cannot let our Catholic faith be blackmailed by any corporation," he continued. "I cannot accept the deception required of our churches. I cannot accept the fact that others who are not of our faith will die because of it. Therefore, I will notify Mr. Lynch of this decision immediately."

The Pope looked around, waiting for feedback on

his announcement. There was none forthcoming until Cardinal Hickey spoke up.

"Your Holiness, please excuse the question, but if we do not accept the offer, is it not understood that they will go to another faith and offer them the same? If the Muslims agree to their terms, what will become of us?"

"Yes, Henry, you are correct, that is probably their next line of communication. However I cannot endure the facade of lies required to perpetrate this "gift" on the Church. If you recall my speech before we started this process about the guidance of God?"

The group silently nodded and the Pope continued.

"I believe that God has selected me for a reason at this particular time in history. I believe that I have been chosen for this task and I awoke this morning convinced of my direction. God has spoken to me, he has shown me the way, and I must honor His decision."

The Cardinals did not know what to do next, some looked at each other, some stared at the ceiling. Cardinal Dulles could not leave without asking the question:

"Holy Father, if I may, why did you ask us here in the first place if you knew that ultimately you would make the decision?"

"Well, Avery, I did not know I would be required to make the ultimate decision. I requested your presence as I felt that we as a group could best decide and I would, therefore, know God's wishes. That was not the case. I believe that God has worked through us to help me make the correct decision and I thank you all for that."

There were no other questions. The Cardinals had anticipated a longer session, but now after half an hour they were returning to their rooms without knowing if they were required any longer. The slow march back provided time for an exchange of thoughts that ranged from surprise to acceptance.

Henry Hickey marched along mindful of his conversation with John Abbott.

Chapter 20

February 27th

"Good afternoon all. First off I want to thank you for agreeing to meet as a group without His Holiness. I would like to discuss something with you that I think would benefit the group as well as our brothers and sisters in faith.

"As you know, the last few days have been eye-opening for all of us and I know that we have a difference of opinion within the larger group." Cardinal Hickey hesitated before continuing.

In the small private conference room off the Hallway of Angels, surrounded by ancient canvases of the life of Christ and the Apostles, the small group of Cardinals listened attentively. Their black and red garments stood out against the fully curtained back wall.

"But I have asked you here because we all voted in favour of accepting the offer from GeneQwest and I believe we can appreciate the Pope's decision and understand it based on the history of our church and the number of people it would affect. It was clear to me, as I am sure that it was to all of you, that he did not have any other option, by his reckoning, but to decline the proposal from GeneQwest. I also believe that we, as a group, must fully support his decision and will, in facing public opinion, join him in defending it. But gentlemen, I want to propose an alternative to his decision.

"To continue, we all know each others' opinion in relation to the matter at hand. I believe that together we can influence the way our faith can grow and prosper. In this room we have three Cardinals that are part of the committee of Cardinals that sit on the board of the Vatican Bank. It is my observation that with their help we can navigate to a different outcome.

"In the interest of expediency, I will get right to it. I would like you to consider accepting GeneQwest's proposal. This will only be known to the people in this room. It will remain in confidence and, if asked, each of us will deny any knowledge of it and will never divulge it happened. I also propose that we counter Mr. Lynch's demand for 3 billion US dollars with an offer of 2 billion." Henry pressed his agenda. Better to go with the quick kill.

Eyes around the room quickly began to search out interest or dissent; years of dealing with parishioners served them well in discovering truth as well as lies.

Cardinal Willebrands was the first to respond. "Cardinal Hickey, what you are suggesting is that we as a group go against His Holiness and, as a result, we go against the word of God. It is heresy! How can you even suggest such a thing?" he said, throwing up his hands.

Two other Cardinals quickly stepped up to reinforce the opinion of Cardinal Willebrands. The room hummed with the low murmurs of voices discussing the new proposal.

"I understand your concern Cardinal Willebrands," Henry responded, raising his voice to be heard above the conversations, "and I do appreciate you pointing out the apparent conflicts. I also have considered this and I feel that we must attend to our consciences to determine how the Lord is directing us. I know that the Pope is our shepherd, but I am of the opinion that the greater good is served by accepting the offer. I also believe that history will show that this is a turning point for humanity. Never before in the history of the church or in fact the history of the world since Christ, has there been a bigger decision. I want to remind everyone that we are talking about human lives. We are dying off, my brothers. One by one, until we are no longer a factor on this planet, we are leaving the world to the unknown. Do you really believe we have done God's work only for Him to abandon us? To let us die? To let the planet dissolve into the abyss? I, for one, believe that God would never do such a thing. He loves us too much."

Cardinal Hickey searched for his glass of water as his mouth was drying up from his speech.

"Is there anyone in this room who truly believes that God would let such a thing happen? Maybe God has given us Gordon Lynch to let us chose our destiny. God has given us free will; this is the ultimate test of that gift."

Silence fell over the room. At the opposite end of the table, Cardinal Dolan stood up.

"Henry, we have known each other for quite some time. I have always believed that being a man of the cloth came with many challenges. I have dealt with several issues in my diocese that came with grave consequences, but I have never been asked to decide on something that has such immense implications for so many. As I said, I have known you for many years. I have seen your commitment and dedication to the church. To ask us to make a decision on such issues, we need time. It is a complex situation, but on the surface, as much as I respect his Holiness, I am in agreement with you, and support you."

"Thank you very much Bill, but I don't think we really have much time. We have to act. We have to decide now."

Cardinal Pappalard spoke up. "What do you believe is the timeline for this decision and what do you see as the consequences if it is discovered?"

"Well, the timeline is now - in fact by end of day. We cannot let this continue. Too many people will be affected."

"What would the consequences be?"

"Well Salvatore, if discovered we may all be excommunicated. It will be the end of our careers, but let me add that it will be the end of us anyway, if we don't try. We must all be in agreement with our verdict; there cannot be any abstaining, or disagreement amongst us. We must all be on side."

"If we agree to such a thing," said Cardinal Pappalard, "how do we go about getting the finances in place to pay Mr. Lynch?"

"I propose that the three members of the group

with us today that sit on the Academy's board use their influence to donate the necessary proceeds to an arm of one of Mr. Lynch's companies that is researching a cure for this latent gene. It will appear that we are helping the cause, and we can negotiate a series of installments."

"And how do we explain it to His Holiness, because, as you know, he will find out?"

"Well Cardinal Dulles, by the time he finds out, it will be too late. Hopefully, in that time we can persuade him to see our point of view. Even if he doesn't agree, he can still make an announcement that the Catholic Church is working with scientists around the world to combat this evil. Remember, once it appears to the masses that the Catholic Church has avoided this plague, his numbers and popularity will soar. I ask you, is there anyone who loses in this scenario?"

Chapter 21

February 28th
Rome, Italy

Celio's bakery in Il Mirot, Rome, had brought notoriety to the area when selected to supply the Vatican with the Eucharist. Armando Celio had been authorized by the Holy See to bake the Eucharist for the last twenty-five years; the generational affair had passed down from father to son for over seventy five years.

The recipe was delivered every year in a small grey envelope stamped with a red-waxed Vatican seal.

Pulling out this year's delivered instructions, he reached for his nearby glasses. They slipped down his nose from sweat due to the bakery's constant heat.

Dear Armando,

Please find enclosed a notice of a revised recipe for the Eucharist. The changes, though minor, will address the changing needs of our parishioners; it will align the Church with the growing issue of food allergies that have come to the forefront in recent years. Please revise your recipe immediately, and as per our confidentially agreement, please do not inform or distribute this to others.

We appreciate your years of dedication to the Catholic faith.

On behalf of His Holiness,
Cardinal Hickey
Vatican City

The same instructions were sent to every bakery producing the host everywhere in the world.

Chapter 22

March 5th
New York City, New York

Rick Johnson and Peter Turner had both started their careers in the old Times building on 42nd Street, working their way up the newspaper ladder to become respected reporters. Now their offices were located in the new Times building, the twisting 52 storey glass tower on 8th Avenue between 40th Street and 41st that was the latest addition to the Manhattan skyline. Their two offices overlooked the pool of junior reporters who were next on the ladder, striving to reach their level.

Rick covered the city beat, always had his ear to the ground, eyes to the sky, tuned into the carryings on in the city. Perennially in touch, he had so many contacts on his iPhone that once a month he had to update his list to make room for the latest celebrity or politician that was making a buzz in New York.

Pete, a wordsmith and an investigative reporter by

nature, headed for the meatier stories that had some regional or international impact on New York and beyond. Wanting to shake things up, he wrote feature pieces that questioned the established norms and opened his readers' eyes to corruption, double dealing and prejudice. Pete's dress code of jeans and a t-shirt, like his attitudes towards fairness and justice, had never changed throughout his career.

Pete had struggled through years as a staff reporter until he finally landed in the feature world. No daily deadlines or editors were screaming at him; he had earned the plum job of selecting his own topics for the Sunday edition. His mandate was to cover stories that he thought would be of interest to the paper's demographics. His editor had given him carte blanche and his experience and writing style provided a combination that readers loved.

Heads down, each reading the latest edition, the pair headed toward the overused, messy coffee room for their morning shot of caffeine.

"Another one! Jesus Christ, these things are like popcorn, they're popping up every six months it seems."

"What the hell are you talking about?" asked Rick.

"These fucking new viruses. We just get over the

bird flu, then Norwalk again, and, I don't know, what the hell was the latest one? Probably some monkey virus that jumps to us. I don't know, seems to me there's a new one every day," replied Pete.

"What's up your ass? You know someone somewhere saves all of us from total annihilation every time. Just write about it and leave it at that," replied Rick.

"Yeah I know, I just get tired of hearing how somebody is infected with some shit, then it creates endless theories and stories that we have to follow and in the end it's never as bad as those so-called experts predicted. You know Rick, sometimes I think they make this shit up just to get their names in the newspaper or on YouTube, you know what I mean?" asked Pete.

"Yeah, sometimes I wonder the same thing. But hey, we are not paid to wonder, we are paid to report the news, so get down to it and put your award-winning skills to the test," Rick said jokingly.

"Yeah, yeah, ok, I got it, just a little fed up, that's all."

"What, did you have a fight with your wife last night?"

"Yeah, that's it, a fight, sure, let's say it's that," Pete answered.

Pete suddenly had an idea for the weekend edition. The topic for his next feature would be 'Viral Attacks – Our Frightening Future or A False Alarm?'.

"So, what the hell are you thinking about now?" asked Rick.

"Well, since you asked, I am wondering about all this crap, I've been following this story on some new virus in St. Lucia. It came over the wire the other day, and now it's getting picked up. Seems there's an outbreak of some kind that's affecting a bunch of locals in Castries. Do you know anything about St. Lucia?"

"Nope, not really. Carla and I went there one year, think it was about 5 years ago or so. Nice place, little backwards, but we were in some resort there. I remember the drinking and bikinis, but that's about it," replied Rick.

"Thanks for that, I guess you would remember those," laughed Pete.

"Remember when it was just shitty coffee that we all complained about?" recalled Rick.

"Yep, sure do, look at all this now. You might as well do your washing at the same time," joked Pete. An upgraded coffee station filled with cappuccino and espresso pods had replaced the old coffee pots but the counter still never stayed clean.

"I know. So are you planning a trip to St. Lucia to check that story out?" asked Rick.

"Not yet, have to do a bit more digging, but it might be in the offing." Pete smiled. "And I know who to talk to if I go."

"Yep, I can point you in the right direction." Rick grinned.

After returning to the glass enclosures that they had nicknamed aquariums, Pete started reading some online web feeds on the virus and its assumed causes and effects. Typing in 'viruses in St. Lucia' on Google brought him almost a million results.

The first link was a week old story in the St. Lucia Voice, 'Outbreak of Virus Contained'. Pete double clicked the headline and began reading a piece from the online newspaper.

To determine the source of the new virus hitting the island, the government has requested additional help from the United States to assist the local medical community in gathering swabs and skin samples from individuals presently infected with the virus. The goal of the coordinated effort is to determine the origin of the virus and understand its genetic makeup in order to create a vaccine to combat its effects.

Presently, we have ten laboratory confirmed cases and three deaths. It is the hopes of this government that we can identify and contain this virus. Our commitment is to the citizens of St. Lucia and to all visitors that we will remain vigilant in our efforts to ensure their health and safety during this time.

Pete emptied the dregs of his coffee cup into his garbage can, banging it on the side of the metal can to make sure it was empty. He put his feet on the edge of his new desk beside his laptop and pondered the wording of the announcement. It was the type of story that tweaked his interest. Newsroom chatter filtered through his aquarium walls like white noise. It helped him to think. Deciding to investigate further, he double clicked on other websites reporting on the outbreak.

Something didn't sit right with him. Tapping his yellow HB pencil on his desk, he roamed the Internet. Since the article in the St. Lucia Voice, the number of deaths had increased to over 50 in a three-week period. It had now made the webpage of the World Health Organization as part of an announcement that they were sending a representative to St. Lucia.

Pete's interest was piqued; it was time to push the envelope. Standing up, he hitched up his jeans and waved to Rick through the glass wall, motioning him to come in to his office. Rick mouthed the words "what for?" but Pete's waving didn't stop. Seeing the excitement of his long time friend, he stuck his head round the door of Pete's office.

"What the hell has got into you, for God's sake?"

"Come and have a look at this. Doesn't this seem strange to you?"

Rick worked his way around the boxes of files stacked around Pete's office, looking at the screen. Pete pointed to some words. Rick scanned the monitor.

"What? What the hell Pete? So what? I think you're losing it my friend."

"Look, every single death certificate on record in St. Lucia that I pulled from the St. Lucia coroner's office has the same thing on them. There's something weird going on. Check out these certificates. I'm just showing you three, but I've pulled up more. What's the one thing that's on all of them?"

"Ok, that's enough, what is it, for Christ sake? I have my own shit to do."

"None of them were Catholic," said Pete.

"Big deal Pete, maybe there aren't many Catholics on the island?"

"Listen Rick, you know I do my homework. Since all this information is in the public domain what I did was, for each person that kicked the bucket, I pulled their birth certificates to see if they were baptized and if so which religion they fell under. So here is the kicker, with a population of around 170,000 on a small isolated island where the majority of people are Catholic, not one - and I mean not one - of the deaths from this virus thing hit them. And to add to this, I have since noticed that the numbers of dead are increasing and again no Catholics. Don't you think that is just a little strange?"

"Ok, my man, maybe a little, but I repeat, big deal."

"Well, it just gets me interested. There's something there, I know it. You and I have been reporters for too long. With the statement from the government plus the U.S. getting in there, now the W.H.O. raising eyebrows... I'm telling you - something stinks," replied Pete.

"So what are you going to do about it?" asked Rick.

"Well I can tell you one thing: I won't be writing

some boring story about another virus. Remember this morning I said I wondered if they just want to get their name in the papers? Well it'll be in the papers all right, I'll make sure of that."

Rick raised his hand as if in disgust. "Whatever my friend, do what you want, but watch out for the hammer, you know what I mean?"

Pete looked at Rick. "Yep, I know what you mean, that hammer has fallen a few times on both of us. I'll watch my back."

Back at the screen Pete kept digging. Over the next two days he scoured the web for more information from different countries and found more hospitalization, more deaths, but not among Catholics. Not one.

It was time to take a trip to St. Lucia.

Chapter 23

From the sidelines the floor director started his finger countdown indicating to all that they were going live in, three...two...one. His index finger pointed directly to his anchor for their morning news show. Intro music rang out on cue as the red light above the camera glowed signaling that they were on.

"Good morning everyone, this is CNN's Starting Point, your early morning news and information show. I'm Alison Riddell."

Behind the camera the floor director orchestrated the stream of information. He was connecting with Alison through her earpiece on what piece was next up and when to go to break. He coordinated his words with a mimicked motion of breaking a tree branch to signal a commercial.

"We will right back after this short break with Mr.

Peter Turner."

"Great Alison," piped the floor manager, "We are back in two."

"Welcome back," smiled Alison, looking directly into camera one after the commercial break.

"With us now is Peter Turner, reporter for the New York Times."

"Good Morning Peter. I understand the piece that you wrote two weeks ago is getting a lot of attention these days."

"Morning Alison. Yes, it is beginning to get lots of eyeballs on it since the original story ran in the Times Sunday edition."

"Can you tell me and our viewers what happened after that?"

"Sure. Well, let's see if I can condense it down. My story was on a new virus, and like the bird flu or Norwalk, people are used to seeing all the normal warnings and precautions, but I approached this one from a different angle. I received emails and tweets from many people, some thinking I was right on, others of course thinking I was crazy, but I have run into that many times, so from there, it was posted on our website and it began to get thousands of hits, which is about normal. Nothing that I didn't expect."

"I also heard that you had a phone call as a result of the articles, is that right?"

"Yes, well, I guess you never know who is reading what these days. I got a phone call from Alan Burgess from the World Health Organization."

"And what was his interest or reason for the call?"

"I figured he wanted to congratulate me on my article, you know making people aware of the health risks out there, stuff like that, but I soon realized it was a bit more than that."

"What do you mean 'more than that'?"

"Well he wanted to meet with me to discuss my research and also my sources."

"Interesting. So Peter at that point did you have any idea about what was about to happen?"

"No, none whatsoever. I've been a reporter for a long time Alison, and I've dealt with many people and organizations that didn't like what I wrote about them, so I figured it was just another one of those cases."

"So when you actually met with Alan Burgess… was that who it was?"

"Yes, that is correct."

"Alan Burgess requests a meeting with you, which

you accepted. Then what happened?"

"At that point it started to get interesting. During the meeting we talked about my knowledge of the subject and what I knew about the local situation, but I sensed a push back, not sure what you would call it… sort of a 'don't go any further with this' feeling. He was a very nice person, extremely professional and cordial, but I've been in this game a long time and I get this feeling, an instinct. It's like tuning a radio to get the right station; I got it at that meeting. It's hard to explain Alison, but you know what it's like when you interview someone and you can sense they're holding back."

Out of camera view, the floor director was again making the break action signaling Alison that they would be cutting to a commercial in under two minutes and she needed to prepare herself and her guest for the break.

"Yes, I think I know what you are referring to. We only have a couple of minutes left before the break, so after your meeting… what happened then?"

"I decided to dig a little deeper into this, antenna up. When someone points me away from a story, I will head right back at it. So I did some follow up and some further investigation, and that is when I wrote the second story. That was the one that lit the fire."

"We have to take a break but we will be back with Peter Turner."

"All good," Alison heard through her earpiece. "We will need to wrap this up in about four minutes when we return."

She nodded and gave a thumbs up to the booth crew.

"Peter, we will have about four minutes after the break. We need to wrap up the story then, can you do it in that time?"

Make-up rushed in to touch up Alison's hair, making sure nothing was out of place. Like bees, they swarmed around her, fussing over their subject until seconds to live air. She was used to this interjection and waited for Peter's answer.

"Sure, four minutes is enough. I'll cut to the chase when we go back on air. Is there anything you want me to do differently?"

"No, not really, I just want you to be aware of our timeline. We believe this is a big story and we will be following it for the next while. We do think this has some longevity to it."

"Well I know it does, I think this is very big - bigger than we imagine."

Waving hands were counting down the time before returning to air – three, two, one…

"We are back with Peter Turner, reporter for the New York Times. He has published two stories that have created quite a stir, not just in this country, but around the world.

"Peter, before the break, we had talked about your meeting with the director at the World Health Organization and his request - or let's say interest - in your first story. What did you discover when you decided to continue with your research?"

"Right. Well, after that meeting I was determined to dig deeper on the subject and I uncovered some interesting patterns with the virus."

"For the viewers just joining us, Peter's story was on a virus that started in St. Lucia and began to spread. At first it wasn't anything that raised eyebrows, but it quickly began to show signs of mutating into something that no one had seen before. Correct Peter?"

"Yes that's right, and that, as I mentioned earlier, was my angle on the story. After meeting with the W.H.O., I uncovered that this virus hits people very hard. Once hospitalized they grow worse and within a couple of weeks they show no signs of recovery. To make matters worse, it begins by affecting their muscles. It kind of locks their muscles up so they can't get up or basically move, and once that hits them they die about a month later."

The news team at CNN flashed images of people in hospital who were hooked to medical machinery. The pictures of human frailty provided an effective backdrop to Peter's words.

"As I understand this, it hits people like a flu virus then mutates or morphs into some other thing?"

"Yes, and it is that other thing that is killing people, but the interesting thing about all this is that it goes one step further. It seems like it affects certain people and not because of their racial or ethnic backgrounds. It's about their religion."

"Just a minute, I want to make sure we are correctly informing our viewers. The virus goes after certain religions? How can that be?"

"No, not certain religions: it hits every religion except Catholics."

"That is quite the statement Mr. Turner. You're saying that this is a virus that does not affect people of a specific faith. Do you stand behind that statement?"

"I know, it was surprising to me as well, and I

think that is why the director came to see me. And yes I stand behind my statement."

"We have about a minute left, what advice do you have for the public in regards to this outbreak?"

"It wouldn't be just one thing. I would just like to make people aware of what is happening. My job is to inform people and I think that this information is important for people to know. There is something going on out there and I've just scratched the surface. I am sure there is more to it than what I have written Alison."

"Thank you for your time and your interesting articles, Peter. I am sure we haven't heard the last of this."

"Thank you Alison."

"Stay with us, up next a story from China."

The floor manager signaled for the commercial break. The camera's red light turned off and people prepared for the next story. The CNN information flow continued.

"So, do you believe that guy Alison?" asked Ron the production manager.

"You know, I've interviewed lots of people Ron. This guy isn't making this shit up. There is something to this story, I'm not sure what, but I think it would be a good thing to keep our eyes on this one. It could lead to bigger fish, especially after that last statement about the Catholics - that will really shake the cage."

Returning to her desk, Alison adjusted the small microphone attached to her dress and waited for the next cue from Ron: three, two, one ...

"We are back, thank you for joining us. This story from Beijing, last night at around 2 o'clock local time...."

Peter left the CNN building and headed back along 8th street to his office. He knew his email would be filling up as he walked.

Chapter 24

March 27th

Gordon paced carefully across the floor of his office. Reaching the window overlooking the Manhattan skyline he peered out for a couple of minutes, thinking hard. A 50-inch TV hanging from the ceiling spat out words but Gordon didn't hear them. The feel of the crumpled cellophane wrapper in his pants pocket reminded him that it was about time for another cigarette.

Returning to his desk, he opened the drawer that contained his cigarettes, gum and various matchbooks from New York's finest restaurants. He pulled out a stick and lit it. Relaxing into his black high back chair, he turned to face the TV.

"Stayed tuned, next up is a reporter with a story you won't want to miss," a voice announced from the wall. "This is CNN."

Taking another haul, he felt the grey smoke fill his lungs. He hung on for as long as he could, and as he exhaled it over his desk, the smoked formed shapes that reminded him of small animals. Gordon never paid attention to the no smoking rules of the building.

"We are back. With us now is Peter Turner, reporter for the New York Times."

The name got Gordon's attention. He had read Turner's piece in the Times and wondered how long it would be before it attracted the media. After listening to the interview, he picked up the remote and switched it off.

A small grin turned up his cracked lips. Everything was falling into place.

Chapter 25

March 28th
Bristol, England

James washed the plates from supper and stacked them neatly to air dry as he did most evenings. The neat and orderly two-bedroom apartment did not have the usual appearance of a single male's domain. Everything was in order: his books arranged by subject matter, magazines stacked by date and no lonely socks left in corners. His second bedroom doubled as his workstation. A desk stood in the corner, home for the two laptops that were waiting for his next command.

Sitting on the couch, wanting to give his steak and kidney pie time to digest, he put his feet up on the coffee table, reached for the remote and the latest *Science* magazine at the same time and turned on his wall-mounted 42 inch flat screen. He was listening for the weather report while flipping through the magazine. He heard the forecast for the next day - rain in the morning -

then a news teaser caught his attention.

"Next on BBC One, a reporter from the New York Times shares with us his claim that the so-called Vatican virus has a religious bias. But first the weather. Lucy, what is happening around the country?"

"Thank you Elizabeth. In London and surrounding areas..."

James waited for the long-winded weather forecaster to finish her countrywide summary of England's climate.

"And now by satellite from New York, Mr. Peter Turner. Thank you for joining us tonight."

"You're welcome; it's good to be here."

"Mr. Turner, I understand that you have been following the path of this virus that has been infecting and in fact killing people on the island of St. Lucia. What can you tell us that we don't already know on this side of the Atlantic?"

"Well, I know that most of you have already heard about or read my articles on the subject, but tonight I want to inform your audience about what I understand to be the latest development on the issue."

"Please do."

"It is now apparent that the first indications I

reported on are correct: we are all being infected by the so-called virus except those of the Catholic faith. But I would also like to make something very clear. What we thought was a virus is actually not a virus. It is a gene mutation. There is a big difference. Viruses can usually be stopped with research and time, but this is not the case in gene mutation. Also, my sources inform me that the discovery was found in the United Kingdom. A lab in your country, I don't know which one, has uncovered this latent gene occurrence."

"Are you telling us now that it has been confirmed that we are not dealing with a virus, in fact we are dealing with something much worse - can we say something unstoppable?"

"Yes, Lucy, I am. I have proof that it is skipping Catholics. They are immune to the gene mutation. This is not a virus. I know it seems far-fetched, but I assure you I have been a reporter for too long to know that if you don't have a reliable source you will be shot down very quickly. My source could not be closer to this issue. As far as unstoppable, I can't comment on that."

"Well, Mr. Turner, that is quite a revelation. Please tell us more."

"Yes, well, I wanted to bring this to light. I

believe that it needs to be out there. If Catholics are being missed by this mutation, then maybe we can use this information to find a cure and save thousands - if not millions - of lives."

"There is no arguing with that. Now you say your source is reliable, can you give us a clue as to this source?"

"Lucy, you know I can't, but I am sure that once this escalates there will be numerous sources."

"So just to summarize our conversation tonight for our viewers, you have proof that the latent gene mutation doesn't affect Catholics."

"Yes, in a nutshell I guess you could say that the latent gene appears to have spiritual preferences."

"Thank you, Mr. Turner, I am sure we haven't heard the last of this. Just one last thing, are you Catholic?"

As the interview ended, the words 'latent gene' echoed in his ears. James picked up the remote and replayed the interview through his PVR. As he watched it again, this time more closely, the New York reporter appeared to be well informed and confident in his source. A sudden panic surged over him; he could feel the anxiety circulating around his body.

He replayed the interview again, this time writing down the name of the reporter. He had to get in touch with him, had to find out more about his source. It was too close to what he had been working on; somehow the secret had escaped the confines of the lab.

Picking up the phone he placed a call into Gordon at GeneQwest, his clammy hands readjusting to get a better grip on the phone.

"Hello," he heard the voice at the other end of the line.

"Hello, Gordon. It's James."

"James, you've caught me at a bad time, I'll call you back at this number, you at home?"

"Right, yes, I am sorry about that, but I needed to chat with you regarding what I just saw on the news."

"Can't this wait for a few hours? I am heading in to an important meeting."

"Right, again, I am sorry about the intrusion, but I need to discuss something with you."

"Ok, ok, I will give you a call right back. This had better be good my friend," snorted Gordon.

"Thank you, I'll be waiting," replied James.

Gordon hung up; shoving his phone in his pant

pocket he headed to the elevator bank for the building where an open door was available. He pressed the 34th floor button to take him up to his meeting. The brass doors opened at the reception area for Shea and Sterling Law firm. Gordon informed the receptionist of his arrival and sat down in the waiting area to call James. He dialed James' number, listening for the mechanical sounding ring.

James picked up immediately.

"Hello, James, Gordon here."

"Thank you for returning my call, and I apologize for the intrusion."

"So what the hell is so important?"

"I just finished watching a report on the BBC with a reporter from the New York Times. He was going on about a latent gene that is mutating and leaving dead people in its wake."

"So, tell me something I don't know. It's been all over the papers here, guess you guys are behind the times."

"No, I understand that, and we do have it in many publications here, but how could he know that this gene mutates and has a selection preference? We are the only ones who know that, and he said that he has a source.

That's impossible. I have never talked to this person." James was panic stricken.

There was silence at the other end of the line. Gordon wondered how long he could remain quiet.

"Gordon, are you there?" asked James.

"Yep, still here. I know that you've never spoken to that guy. Would there be anyone from your team that might have let it slip, maybe after a few drinks?"

"No way. In fact there is no one who knows about it - it is just you and I that know what's going on here. My team is working on other projects."

"Are you sure no one else knows about it?"

James hesitated replaying the history of events in his mind.

"Well, there is one other person, but she would never make the connection."

"And who would that be?" asked Gordon.

"Sara, Sara Smith."

"Ok, James, before you explode let me explain something to you. Sometimes in business you have to create a buzz, an interest. You know like a trailer to a movie, it gets asses in seats, you know what I mean?"

"Sort of, but I'm not sure how this relates to what we are talking about."

"Let's just say that I might have let it slip about what GeneQwest has been working on."

"'Let it slip'? What do you mean?"

"I told that guy, Peter Turner, what was happening. Sort of."

"You what? Why would you do that? And what do you mean sort of? We are not one hundred percent sure that it *does* have a selective process. We know that it's killing people, but to go so far as to say that it's protecting Catholics… that is a bit of a stretch."

"James, indirectly we will be helping the world. Think about it - from behind the scenes we will be monitoring the gene's progress, and let's face it, it sure looks like it doesn't like Catholics. You know you have the solution to the selective scenario, so now all we do is get it to the rest of the world as soon as possible and this gene mutation thing will be defeated and all will return to normal," replied Gordon.

"That sounds good in theory, but I get the impression that somehow it's made its way into Catholic hands and they are keeping for themselves."

"James, that's crazy. Do you know what would happen if that were true? We would have some kind of religious war or at least some sort of backlash."

"I... I don't know what to say. How else could this be viewed?"

"Remember, you work for me. We had a business arrangement. Have you ever wanted for anything?"

"No, Gordon, I haven't, but I don't think that this should have been announced through the press," James replied, his voice tense with stress.

"Don't worry; all I've done is to start the ball rolling. We will still be doing good work behind the scenes. There is an arrangement I have set up that will keep us undercover. It is best for all parties. I'll tell you what, I am heading over to Bristol in the next couple of weeks for my meds. We'll sit down and chat about it, but right now I need get to my meeting, so let's leave it here," replied Gordon.

"I don't think this can be left for two weeks. I think you should head over here sooner. We need to discuss this. I feel that there other things at play, I'm just not sure what they are right now."

"James, calm down, everything in time. In two weeks I will be there and we will have a good talk about how things will play out and your involvement. Now go back to your TV and watch something else."

"Right, so I will just sit here and wait for you to

arrive."

"That's the plan; see you in two weeks. Bye James."

James listened for the buzzing disconnect sound at the end of the line and hung up the phone. Worried, he paced his apartment like an expectant father; he didn't like the direction this was heading in.

The next morning, as predicted on the weather report, the rain had started to fall early as if it was coordinated with the morning rush. Equipped with his rain slicker and waterproof boots, James pedaled his familiar route down Marsh Street past the shopping plaza.

After thirty minutes of riding his dark blue trousers were soaked from knee to ankle. Arriving at the lab, he wheeled his wet bike onto the concrete floor to an area where it could drip dry. Slicker in hand, the water under his boots squeaked along with him as he moved toward his office. He took off his boots and put on his comfortable brown Clarks.

The ding of email notifications rang out several times until James moved the wireless mouse, clearing away the screen saver.

Chapter 26

A lone desk lamp shone like an oasis of light in the darkened offices of Illumina Labs. Armed with a glass of whiskey and his laptop, James pored over the reports that were being posted with increasing frequency on the World Health Organization website.

Further evidence of the effects of the mutant gene was being documented daily and the information on where and how it was spreading around the globe was chilling. James scrolled down the list of countries where the mutant gene was having the greatest impact. Religious denomination, which now appeared to be a serious consideration, appeared as a subset in each country with percentage numbers displayed for each religion.

A real time computer model showed the estimated creep of the media coined "Vatican Gene" on the planet based on present numbers. The coloured model spread like spilled ink bleeding into paper. Areas of interest flashed on the screen indicating sections where the mutant gene was not having as much of an effect. They were tied to bar charts showing the religious preference by population.

The tie-in was evident to James; he could see that Gordon's plan was working. He knew he had to dig further into the information on the website to find something. He just didn't know what he was looking for.

As he placed his empty glass down, the wet ring on the desk reflected back at him. He told himself that drink was the last he would have for the evening. James leaned in for another look at the screen, feeling the effects of the whiskey. As he thought about how Gordon had twisted his discovery into a bargaining chip and how his antidote was being misused, he knew what he had to do.

He was going over the reports on the website again trying to find the information that would show him a path forward when his cell phone rang. Looking down at the name on the screen he saw it was Sara.

Bringing the phone to his ear he answered, "Hello Sara, you alright?"

"Just sitting here at the pub waiting for you."

"Oh, shit, I'm sorry."

"Yes, don't you remember, we had discussed this at lunch?"

"Yes, I do. What can I say? I'm sorry. Is it too late?"

"No, if you come now I'll wait, but I mean now. I have been waiting here for an hour; I think I have been patient enough, don't you?"

"Absolutely, I will close this up and be right there. Five minutes, give me five minutes and I'll buy you a drink."

"You're on, five minutes."

"Cheers, see you shortly," James said, finishing the call.

Shutting down as quickly as he could, he closed the numerous tabs he had open on his computer. The final screen showed recent religious research relating to genetic consistencies. Reading the research as fast as he could, he saw that it quoted studies on a new theory in molecular genetics, the God Gene. He remembered his deadline with Sara, bookmarked the web page, grabbed his light jacket and hurried to the pub.

Sara was somewhat mollified as she watched him dash into the pub.

"I'm so sorry, my mind was elsewhere," he said

distractedly.

"You're forgiven, even though you are well past your five minutes."

"I am? I must be close though."

"Good enough, I guess," joked Sara.

"Ok, well, let me get you that drink I promised. What would you like?"

"I will have the same as I am drinking now, nice dry wine."

"Right, I'll be right back with that," James replied, wondering if the three drinks plus a pint of lager would have much effect on him.

Sitting back at the table with Sara after buying the drinks, James finally relaxed in his chair.

"So James, what kept your attention at the lab?" questioned Sara.

"Long complicated story, Sara, long story," James said taking a big swig of beer.

"Well, we have some time now. James, let me ask you, with all the panic in the world these days, do you think it is really as bad as the media is making out? We see stuff everyday about the effects of MG-J12 or the so called "Vatican Gene" on the world. Do you think it's as bad as they say?"

James hesitated as he weighted up the alternatives. Keeping things to himself had taken a toll on him and even though he knew that the alcohol was working its way through his bloodstream, the need to talk was overcoming his willpower.

"Well actually, I believe that it's even worse than what the media is telling us."

"What?" replied Sara, "What makes you say that?"

He ran a hand through his brown hair, stalling for time. Hoping he was doing the right thing he decided to tell Sara everything.

"Sara, if I told you what I know, do you think that you can keep it to yourself?"

"Geez, you are scaring me a bit. What the hell are you talking about?"

"It goes back a few months, but I just want to make sure you are ok with hearing what I am about to tell you."

"Well, I'm not sure I can be ok with something that I don't even know about yet."

"Right, let me rephrase that. If we sit here and I tell you all the things I know, you will be involved. Are sure you want to know?"

"What do you mean by involved? Involved in

what? If it's lab stuff, we're doing research for good reasons. Are you doing something criminal or unethical?" Sara asked with concern.

"No, not really, but it's not heading in the right direction and there is no turning back. I have to continue."

"Ok, James, I can't believe you would do anything that would be that corrupt or unscrupulous, so I'll bite. Tell me what's going on."

Looking around the dimly lit pub, with its usual crew of boisterous locals, blissfully unaware of the dangers awaiting them, James felt the last barrier drop. He had to tell someone what was happening just in case something happened to him.

"Sara, we are in an impossible situation. I have been involved in something truly unethical without even knowing that I was. I have been coerced into something that I've had to continue with and now I am trying to figure out an exit plan."

"James, what the hell are you talking about? What situation?"

"Well, to call it onerous would be putting it mildly. Let me start at the beginning."

"Always a good place," Sara replied, looking

apprehensive.

"It all started with that tissue sample from Montana."

"Are you going to tell me that the thing was not a tissue sample from a T-Rex? I thought you put that to bed a while ago."

"No, it was a T-Rex sample, but that was the just the start of more investigation, don't you remember?"

"Vaguely. I knew you were going to solve the problem, but that was the last I heard of it."

Looking over at Sara, James watched the blood drain from her face. She stared directly at him without blinking and sat motionless for what seemed like minutes as the importance of what he was saying sank in.

Finally she said in a quiet voice, "James, are you confirming that nature had a predetermined time for us to go, and this is what we are seeing all around the planet?"

"In a nutshell, yes. We are going extinct."

"Ok, hold on a minute." Sara put her wine glass down. "So there is no way of stopping this thing. This is evolution at work and all we can do is sit back and watch?"

"Well, there's more."

"Right, so what else is at work here?"

"I found a way of stopping this gene. I actually discovered a 'cure' I guess you could call it, but here's the problem. You know who finances all our research, don't you?"

"Yes, it's Illumina. It's on our pay stubs."

"Right, Illumina is on our pay stubs, but we're actually a subsidiary of GeneQwest out of New York. They have kept our work quiet and the ownership of what I discovered rests with them."

"Ok, so what, they own it. They will release the antidote and save the world and everyone will love them."

"Well, that's not going to happen. They are keeping it to themselves," replied James.

"What? That's crazy; they could make billions with that. What would motivate them to keep it quiet?"

"Ok, remember, I said it's a long story. This is where it becomes longer."

"I'm all ears," Sara said intently.

"The CEO of GeneQwest decided to offer it to the highest bidder, a religious bidder to be exact, and you know who won."

"Don't tell me...it can't be."

"Yes, you're right. The Catholic Church. So you see the dilemma."

"Holy shit James, this is crazy. It's nuts. We have to tell someone."

"We can't. I think we would both be in danger if we tried. Gordon would stop at nothing to keep control of the antidote. It gets worse."

For the next hour, James and Sara huddled over the table deep in conversation. James' relief at finding someone he could tell and who understood his work made him want to tell Sara every detail of the research he was doing.

As Sara took in all the information she realized what it had taken for James to put his trust in her.

"So now you can understand the situation that I'm in."

"Yes, I think I do. Do you have any idea what you're going to do about it?"

"Regrettably yes, but I can't tell you anything. It would be too dangerous for you."

"Ok, great, you explain probably the most devastating situation humanity has ever had to face and then tell me you can't tell me anything else. Do you really think that I'm going to leave it at that?"

"Yes, I'm asking you to just leave it at that. You

can maybe help me in other ways, but not in what I plan to do."

"Are you hearing yourself?'

"I guess it does sound confusing, but you're just going to have to trust me."

"Well, I guess I'll have to, now that you've pretty much put your life in my hands. Lucky for you, I'm getting kind of fond of you."

James felt the colour rushing to his cheeks and he looked around the room trying to find a spot he could focus on. His head was spinning a bit and he wasn't at all sure that it was only the alcohol that was at fault.

"Thanks Sara, I know I've been absorbed in my work, but I always thought that we could talk, even though we're discussing the end of the world," James said, only half joking.

"Yes I agree. It would have been better with a different subject," blurted Sara.

"I'll try to pick a lighter subject next time."

"I'm glad to hear there's going to be a next time."

"I'm going to do my best to make sure there are lots of them," James said looking into her eyes. James then pointed in the direction of the washroom. "Be right back, have to run to the loo, then we can leave."

"Sure, I'll be right here," smiled Sara.

Making sure James was out of sight, Sara grabbed her cell phone from her purse and quickly composed a short text.

New information, tell you later. She hit the send button.

"Ready?" James said as he approached their table.

"Absolutely, lead the way."

Sara followed in James's footsteps, leaving the pub.

Chapter 27

April 9th
CNN Headquarters, New York City

"Good afternoon and welcome to Press Room. This is where we ask the tough questions, the questions you'd like to ask. My name is Rod Lewis.

"We would like to follow up on an interview by Alison Morgan of CNN with the lead doctor for the World Health Organization. Dr. Salter has been closely following the situation that Mr. Turner spoke about."

"Dr. Salter, welcome to Press Room."

"Thank you."

"Dr. Salter, let me start right in, can you confirm that you did meet with Mr. Turner recently?"

"Yes, I did meet with Mr. Turner a few months ago, and in regard to the claims Mr. Turner spoke about on CNN, I believe that he is mistaken in his assumptions. We have never seen nor do we have reason to believe that this virus skips Catholics. There is no medical evidence that this is the case. It can be attributed more to chance than to religious affiliation. There has never been any precedent or example of such a claim in the history of the World Health Organization."

"But isn't it a fact, Dr. Salter, that not one person of the Catholic faith has been affected by this virus?"

"Yes, but that does not mean that the assumption Mr. Turner put forth is correct. There is no correlation between this virus and religious persuasion. I would also like to point out that we are not certain that we are dealing with a gene mutation as Mr. Turner described it; it could be something else."

"Then how can you explain the fact that Catholics are not affected?"

"Well, right now I cannot explain, and let me clarify our statement: it is not a fact, it is speculation."

"I understand. So what are you doing to disprove Mr. Turner's claim? Surely there is something you can tell us that will outline the efforts of the WHO in dealing with this issue."

"Certainly. Firstly, we are not out to disprove any claims from any one person, our focus is on the health issue. We have protocols that move us to declare a pandemic situation, and I can assure you that we are not there yet. Our investigators are on site right now, in many areas around the world, reporting their findings. From there we will take the appropriate action."

"It sounds to me like your protocol is getting in the way of the truth."

"Let me assure you that our organization cares only about the truth – the truth about health issues. We look beyond borders and political situations. Our protocol will never get in the way of truth, on that we stand firm."

"Ok, I understand your mandate. I want to leave our viewers with one statement on your behalf that will assure them of your efforts. Would you like to tell us what that would be?"

"Let me assure your viewers that we are doing everything to identify, contain and eradicate this virus. We have handled situations of this magnitude before and our record speaks for itself."

"Thank you, Dr. Salter. There you have it. We will look forward to the results of Dr. Salter and his team in addressing this problem. Stay tuned for more on this story as it develops. This is Rod Lewis, signing off. Stay tuned for Anderson Cooper."

Chapter 28

In the following weeks, Pete Turner gave dozens of interviews requested by international news organizations that began to stir the cauldron of religious bias. Media outlets created hypothetical scenarios based on the frightening new reality. "Should you become a Catholic?" was a favorite theme. The Times in London carried a story on the likelihood of other exclusions in nature and the Washington Post interviewed a geneticist and virologist who were investigating Pete Turner's claims. Bloggers fanned the fire and YouTube videos by conspiracy theorists and religious zealots began to go viral. Right wing politicians got traction from weekly promises to follow the word of God in their leadership platforms. At the World Health Organization and the Centre for Disease Control, teams toiled night and day trying to create a vaccine while ignoring any link to religion.

Dr. Salter instructed his team to investigate all potential outbreaks no matter how insignificant. He quickly grew tired of defending his position and addressing headline-hunting reporters and delegated his most senior media savvy representative to handle all requests. This freed up his time to follow the virus and its effects.

His office door never closed properly. The hinges needed adjusting. Dr. Salter pushed it closed in a fit of annoyance. The crest of the W.H.O. stared back at him from his laptop screen saver. Pressing the keyboard, he pulled up the names of his regional representatives from the six world regions, from Africa to the Americas. Every corner was covered. It was time to advise his people on a course of action. His email message read:

As I am sure you are aware, the situation regarding MG-J12 has escalated. I must remind you that our goal at the W.H.O. is to identify, notify and educate the affected populations with respect to any outbreaks. As the authority under the United Nations, we must provide leadership in the handling of such issues. As we base all notifications on solid evidence and research, I am requesting your most up-to-date regional data. We are facing a severe problem and we must be confident before releasing any information about its impact and consequences. Once again, I stress the importance of coordination and communication on this issue.

> *Thank you,*
> *Dr. Salter, PhD*

Finishing the letter, he pressed the send button. Picking up a red pen just to the left of the picture of his family, he chewed the already crumpled end. The phone rang for the hundredth time. He hesitated while it rang four times; one more ring and voicemail would kick in.

"Hello, Salter speaking," he answered just before the last ring.

"Hello, Dr. Salter, I am calling from the Vatican. Can you please hold for the Pope?"

"Um, yes, certainly." Dr. Salter gripped the phone's handle tightly, composing himself.

"Good afternoon, Dr. Salter. This is Pope John, may I have a word with you?"

Minutes seemed to pass before Dr. Salter replied. "Yes certainly, Your...Holy...Your Holiness."

"First of all, I would like to thank you for all the work you and your team have done in handling the issue of this new strain of virus. Our two organizations have had some disagreements in the past; our position on birth control, for example, has always been in line with the teachings of the Church. I know you think differently. As you know from all the worldwide media attention, people are of the understanding that if you are Catholic you are being bypassed by this deadly condition. My call is two-fold, first of all, to let you know that here at the Vatican, we have done some preliminary research at the Pontifical Academy of Sciences and we can find no correlation between religious belief and genetic mutation."

"Well thank you, Your Holiness; I appreciate your understanding of the matter and I'm glad to hear that the Academy is debunking this thesis. As you know, it is our mandate to research anything that affects world population. It is in this regard that we can agree with your research: there is no correlation whatsoever."

"I do understand your mandate and efforts. The second part of my inquiry is to tell you that we would like to assist you in moving forward. I will open the Academy to any of your researchers. They can benefit from our ongoing efforts and also work together with us in combating this mutation."

"Well, thank you very much, Your Holiness." Dr.

Salter's quiet voice quivered with reverence in spite of himself. "I will notify our team to get in touch with the Academy and I am looking forward to a resolution within a short time with efforts from both organizations. Thank you again."

"You are welcome Dr. Salter. Someone will be in touch with you very soon to begin the process. Goodbye."

"Goodbye, Your Holiness."

Placing the receiver back in its place, Dr. Salter tried to grasp the importance of the call while his mind raced with scenarios. The Pope had never contacted any member of W.H.O. for any reason. He listened to the light rain hitting his window that faced the Hudson River on the 14th floor of the United Nations building, pondering the possible motive behind the call.

Chapter 29

June 4th
Bristol, England

Glancing up from his keyboard, James watched as Sara prepared to shut down for the evening. He was able to see her screen and he waited until her monitor went black before heading out of his office, timing it perfectly to meet her as she headed for the door.

She waved and pulled her handbag strap over her shoulder.

"Goodnight James, see you tomorrow," she said, opening the door.

James picked up his pace and was now within talking distance.

"Sara, can I ask you a question before you scoot home?"

"Sure."

"You know we have worked together for a while now. I was just wondering…"James hesitated, looking down on his brown shoes and feeling his hands getting moist.

"Listen Sara, I am not very good at this stuff, so bear with me. I was wondering if you'd like to go out for a drink, just casual, no pressure, maybe we could just chat about work or something?" James said nervously.

"James, don't worry, you're doing fine. I would love to go out and have a drink. When were you thinking?" Sara asked.

"How about tonight, I could meet you somewhere?" James replied.

"Well… You sure don't give a girl much time to get ready."

"Right. Sorry about that. How about tomorrow then?" James asked.

"Tonight's fine. Just give me a bit to get ready and I will meet you down at the Hatchet in… let's say two hours from now, so that will make it 7 o'clock."

"Excellent, I'll stay at the lab, so it will be no problem. I don't need much time to get ready," joked James.

"Ok then, see you soon." Sara laughed and headed out the door.

James leaned back on his heels, congratulating

himself for asking.

Two hours later James and Sara sat across from each other at the Hatchet. The early hour left plenty of tables to choose from. James felt as though his awkwardness was taking up its own space at the table. He was aware it was more like a date.

"Well it certainly has been a busy time lately," James began.

"Yes it has, but I like it that way. The day passes quickly," Sara replied.

"It sure does, where does the time go?"

Their conversation stalled as they hunted for a common topic.

"Sara, what is it you like to do away from the lab?"

"James, you know, I've told you before, remember?"

He rummaged through his brain to find the corner of his memory where the answer was stored.

"Horses?" His tone was somewhat questioning and unsure.

"Right. Was that a guess?"

"No, I remembered, just had to dig a bit for it."

He smiled.

"So let me ask you, what do you do for fun James?"

Looking around the room James had to think for a moment, "I guess you could say I am a bit of a homebody. I enjoy reading and - now don't laugh - I also enjoy paint by numbers."

Resisting a smile, Sara pushed her empty wine glass forward. "Are you serious, paint by numbers?"

"Well you didn't laugh, but I can tell you wanted to," James said. "I enjoy the mindless release after constantly staring at the screen all day. It kind of relaxes my brain and at the end I have a beautiful picture of a tiger or country barn or some deer in the woods."

Looking at each other they both started to laugh at the same time. Their awkwardness disappeared immediately.

"Another wine?"

"That would be nice."

"I'll be right back."

The pub was beginning to fill up with its regular patrons. Groups congregated in corners and at tables as if they were at home. Waiting at the bar, James glanced around noticing the historic bric-a-brac.

A television in the corner blurted out significant news stories from around the world. A story caught his ear and he glanced up to catch the picture, hoping Sara wouldn't mind.

Lined up, smiling for the camera, fifteen men and women stood in front of the Academy of Sciences at the Vatican. Pub chatter drowned out the TV commentary.

James fixed on the delicate Irish features of one face he recognized; it was Heather Duncan from Dublin. During the semester that she spent at Cambridge they had shared many an evening together discussing the future of genetic development. James had fond memories of time spent with her. He had often wondered where she ended up.

Trying to lip-read the announcer's words over the clamor, James deciphered that this was the team that the Vatican had put together to solve the crisis. Heather stood surrounded by the top scientists from around the world.

"Here you go mate," shouted the bartender, "That'll be six pound fifty."

"Right, sorry, here you go, keep the change."

"Cheers mate."

James walked back to the table with drinks in

hand.

"Here you go Sara." He handed her the wine.

"Thanks James, so where did we finish?"

"Um, painting, you were laughing at my paint by numbers."

"No I wasn't, I would never do that," smiled Sara.

"Ok then, one of these days I'll show you my etchings."

"I look forward to that." Sara said as she sipped her wine.

Their conversation continued for the next two hours, covering various subjects interjected with more alcohol. Much to James's surprise Sara revealed that she was married for about a year back in the States, something he would have never guessed. Just wasn't the right fit she had told him.

The evening was a pleasant surprise for both of them.

"Figure it's time we packed it in for the night?" asked James.

"I guess we should, we do have work tomorrow."

"Come on, let me walk you to your car." He offered his arm.

"Well, that is very gentlemanly of you, James."

She threaded her arm into his as they left the pub, heading in the direction of her car.

As they walked it was evident to James that Sara was not fit to drive. The way she steadied herself against his arm suggested to James a new strategy was needed.

"Sara, I believe I should get you a taxi. Let's just turn around and grab one that's outside the pub."

"That would probably be a good idea."

"You can always pick up your car tomorrow after work."

"What about you James? Oh right, you have your bike."

He smiled. "Goodnight Sara, I enjoyed tonight."

"I did too James, I did too," she said as he opened the taxi's door. "See you tomorrow."

James watched as the taxi drove away, red taillights fading into darkness.

Turning away, James felt the effects of the night's alcohol. Taking deep breaths of the cool night air, he unlocked his bicycle. He reminded himself to look up Heather on the Internet in the morning.

Chapter 30

June 5th

The black Bentley glided to a stop in front of Illumina's nondescript door. His first step out of the back seat landed Gordon in a small puddle on the pavement that had accumulated from last night's rain. Salty sea air hit his nostrils like a wave. Stretching further on the next step he avoided the water and turned in frustration to his driver.

"Seems like every time I come over here it's raining or has just rained. Do you guys every get any sun in is this place?"

"Yes sir we do, last week was lovely, only two days of a bit of rain. But it is nice and green, good for the soul," the man replied.

"Good for the soul, yeah I'll bet. If by soul you mean fish," joked Gordon.

"Yes, that'd be it sir," smiled his driver.

"Ok, listen, I'll phone you when I'm ready. I'm

not sure how long this will take."

"Right you are sir, just give me a ring and I will be right round."

"Good, thanks, see you later," Gordon said, heading for the door.

Touching the peak of his grey cap his driver gave a nod of acknowledgement.

Glancing at his watch as he pushed the door open, Gordon entered the revamped warehouse. Quickly swiping his feet across the doormat, he noticed the water stain that James' bicycle had left on the floor.

Continuing into the main part of the building he was quickly spotted by the research team. Pulling themselves up from their slumped seating positions, they attempted to look professional.

Diffused fluorescent lights hung from the open ceiling, spreading the light gently to the workspace below. Walking with authority, Gordon headed directly to James' office, his overcoat billowing behind him like a cape. He nodded to the onlookers gawking at him as he passed. They all knew who he was. In front of James's office he knocked and, without waiting for any response, he walked straight in.

"Good afternoon James." Gordon's deep voice

echoed off the cement block walls.

Looking up, James was surprised to see his American boss.

"Hello Gordon, are you early or did I not get the time right?"

"Nope, I am an hour early, good tailwind and not much traffic on that M something, don't know the number."

"M4," interjected James.

"Right, 4. So look, I'm on New York time, little hungry, jet lagged, how about you and I take off and get something to eat? I need to talk to you anyway, so we can kill two birds with one stone."

"Sure, that would be fine, just let me close down this file."

"Speaking of stones on the way from the airport I heard some radio guy talking about stones. What is it with you Brits? What the hell is it with this stone shit? He was talking to some woman about her weight, I mean, what's with that? You guys need to get with the times."

"Yes, we still use stones. It's our history; it stays with us I guess." James wondered where this was going.

"It sure does. For what reason, I will never figure that out."

"Well, it gives us a sense of time and place. How old is America?" James asked, pretending innocence.

"I don't know, two hundred, two hundred and fifty, not sure, doesn't make any difference does it. It's done, we can never go back," Gordon replied gruffly.

"I guess not," said James.

"So, where are we going? I'm getting hungry."

"Oh, no problem, just around the corner is a good pub. It won't be too busy right now, so we should have no worries." James got up from his chair.

"Good, I'll follow you."

Gathering his coat, James headed for the door, following Gordon's previous route. After the door closed behind them, the staff breathed a collective sigh of relief and relaxed back down.

As they walked to the Hope and Anchor the sky was clouding over and wind from the east began to blow as it usually did around that time of day, cupping the street litter around into circles.

"So, is this place any good?" asked Gordon.

"Yes, I quite enjoy it. Their fish and chips are the best in the city."

"Great, let's get in there before we get rained on,"

Gordon said, looking up.

The Tudor style building with its whitewashed facade and black trim stood out proudly amongst the other, more run down shops. Its triple peaked roof added some architectural features to an otherwise flat streetscape. Being the oldest pub in Bristol, it hung its bragging rights on a sign close to the entrance door. Established in 1606, it had served some of history's most notorious characters and today it served fifteen types of real ales brewed locally. Pointing out the signage to Gordon as they walked in, James headed for the small round table for two near the thick glass leaded windows.

"How's this?" asked James.

"Looks good to me," replied Gordon.

Sitting down, both James and Gordon removed their coats and spread them on the backs of their wooden chairs.

James stood up again. "So what do you want to drink?"

"What, so you're the waiter too?" questioned Gordon.

"Well in pubs, the way it works is that we go to bar to order. So I'll get the drinks going and then we'll figure out what to eat when I bring back the menu,"

James said, getting ready to head to the bar.

Gordon grimaced. "Ok, whatever, I'll have a dark beer. I'll leave it up to you as I don't have a clue about what's good."

"Right then, I'll get you something I think you'll like."

Returning with two pints of amber-colored ale, James sat down and pushed a large glass in front of Gordon. Picking up his glass, James motioned to Gordon. "Cheers Gordon, good to see you."

"Same goes for me," Gordon replied, knocking their glasses together.

Taking a sip of the amber ale, Gordon quickly picked a meal to order as his hunger narrowed the options. James got up again and placed the order with the barman. He returned to the table quickly, anxious to hear about any new developments at GeneQwest that Gordon was willing to share.

"So, James, I wanted to talk to you, to fill you in as to what's been happening on the other side of the Atlantic, and on a few other developments I have in the works. When you called the other day, I might have given you the wrong impression," Gordon said.

"Yes, sorry about that inconvenience. It just

upset me a bit when I saw that person on television before you told me about what was going on," James said, and took a sip of his beer.

"Right, totally understandable on your part. I came over here to tell you in person what is going on. It is a little different than what you originally signed up for, but I think in the long run you will understand my position."

James moved back in his chair with his arms folded. "So what are we talking about Gordon?"

"Well let me explain, rather than beat around the bush," Gordon replied. "James, you were right. I have cut a deal - the first of many. Your antidote is right now in the hands of only one organization, the Catholic Church. I made them an offer and they have agreed that it is in their best interest to have exclusive rights to this antidote. What that fucking reporter is saying is true, even though he is getting a bit too close for his own good. I gave him the information, not all of it, but just enough to get some interest flowing. As you know, since you discovered the fucking thing, this gene mutates and triggers the same thing that happened to those dinosaurs, so you know that everyone without the antidote is headed for the same outcome."

James felt a knot in his stomach; he interjected before Gordon could continue. "Gordon, hold on, you know and I know what was supposed to happen. I work for you but you told me that with this discovery we could make a difference to the world, basically save people's lives. Are you telling me that we, I mean you, are not doing that?"

"Hold on James, let's not get your pants all twisted," replied Gordon.

"Twisted? They're strangling me! What the hell is going on? What about all the people that are not Catholics? They are faced with a certain death; do we just sit around and watch?"

"They will get their turn. Right now this is easy; no other religion gives their believers something to swallow every Sunday. The cure is in the Eucharist, they just don't know it. So, right now the Catholics have the use of the antidote. They will be using it for a year or two, and then it will go to some other group." Gordon took another sip of his beer.

"Some other group? Who selects the 'other' group?" James asked making air quotes with his fingertips.

"Well, I select them and it depends."

"Depends on what?" retorted James.

"Money, it depends on money James. Money."

"So are you telling me that whoever gives you the most money gets to live?"

"If you put it that way, I guess, yes." Gordon said with a smirk.

"Who ordered the fish and chips?" the smiling waitress asked.

Gordon slightly raised his hand. "Right here, honey."

"And the steak and kidney pie must be for you?" she said.

"Yes, that's right, thank you," James said distractedly.

"Can I get you anything else, brown sauce, vinegar?"

"How about some ketchup dear?" asked Gordon.

"Sure. Be right back," replied the waitress.

She returned and placed the ketchup on the table before turning to handle a request from another table.

"Gordon, do you know what you're doing?" James asked as he absentmindedly chipped at the pastry-topped pie with a fork.

"Yes, James, I do. It will be fine, it will work out, everyone will get a turn, and everyone will be saved - well, except for those who don't get the antidote in time. In the meantime we and the Catholics with their new found followers are making a few bucks. What is so wrong about that?" Gordon asked.

"What's wrong?" James said with a dry laugh. "Are you kidding me? The whole thing reeks of corruption and power mongering."

"And your point is James?"

"My point is that it *is* wrong. Pure and simple. Wrong." James was suddenly unable to stomach the sight of his steak and kidney pie.

"James, come on, wake up and smell the world. Money makes it go around and if you don't make money you can't help anybody or anything. Here you are living in this nice little British town, you've buried yourself in research and lost touch with how you get paid. Do you think I just go to the bank and ask for money? The bank wants to see the flow of cash keep coming. What we are doing is just business, it is done more often than you care to think about," Gordon said in a condescending voice.

"I don't want to think about it right now," replied James. "I am just stunned, Gordon, I really don't know what to say."

"You don't have to say anything, just keep doing

what you're doing and everything will be fine. And by the way, don't get any ideas of telling anyone this shit, because I will just deny it and you will be out of a job and millions of people will die. So you see my friend, you are between a rock and a hard place. That leak to the reporter was just a set up to increase awareness and to get the numbers up in Catholic churches. He doesn't know that we are actually saving lives. Come on, finish your beer and we can go back to the lab and I can get my meds. As you guys say over here, chin up," Gordon said laughing.

James quickly gulped down the remainder of his drink, stood up, grabbed his coat from the back of the chair and headed for the door. Gordon followed close behind.

James walked with his head down, staring at the pavement. Gordon could tell that he was mulling over his options.

"Come on, James," he said gently, "When you stop and think about what we're doing, we really are saving people, they just don't know it."

James turned to look Gordon square in the face. "Are we really saving mankind from extinction or just from itself?"

"What the hell are you talking about? Sometimes, James, you think too much. It's black and white; we are saving people from a certain death. How can that be a bad thing? The byproduct is just a little cash flow for GeneQwest."

James didn't answer. Arriving at the door to Illumina he turned to Gordon and said in a neutral voice, "Come on in and I'll get you your medication."

"Ok, that's better James. You'll see. It will all work out in the end," Gordon said patting James on the back.

"Maybe Gordon, maybe. What if something goes wrong?"

"Nothing is going to go wrong, no one can say anything to anyone, too many asses are on the line," Gordon replied with a sidelong glance at James.

"I suppose so." James handed Gordon his dose for the next month.

"Just remember, Gordon, this is experimental stuff. I don't know the extent of side effects or the long term implications. You have been on it now for seven months or so. It is controlling the growth of your cancer, but it might have side effects that I am not aware of. Might want to think about easing off a bit," James said.

"There you go again, worrying. Hey, it's working for me, and that's all I know or care about right now. Just remember, James my man, the future is so bright we have to wear shades. Well over here you wouldn't know what I mean - you never get any fucking sun," Gordon said jokingly.

"Yes, you're right Gordon, never any sun," James replied, looking at Gordon with a tight smile.

Medication in hand, Gordon made a call to his driver.

"All ready my man."

"Alright sir, I'll be there in a couple of minutes. I am just around the corner."

"Ok, James, it was a quick visit but I figured you should know what was happening. I have a few more business issues in London tomorrow, and then I am out of here the next day, so I will be talking to you when I get back. I'll keep you in the loop on any new developments, but I don't expect any. All the wheels on the bus are rolling in the same direction now. It's too late to get off." Gordon said making a spinning motion with his hands.

Gordon caught sight of the Bentley's nose appearing around the corner.

"Got to go James, car is here, talk to you soon."

He shook James's hand with a firm grip.

"Right then, have a safe trip back," James replied waving goodbye.

Gordon's car door was open, awaiting his entrance. As he stepped inside, his driver closed the door, nodding goodbye to James.

James watched the black Bentley swing into the narrow road, searching for the M4.

Chapter 31

Television cameras perched on tripods swiveled into position via remote control with the precision of a ballet. In the control booth the producer sat ready to put the Vatican's communications arsenal to use and communicate with the world. His name was Alfred Sissoori and after years at the helm of Vatican Productions, he was the trusted manager of the message. Impeccably groomed with grey flannel trousers and light blue shirt with white onyx cuff links, he smiled as the Pope entered the room.

The Pope smiled back. "Hello Alfred," he said.

"Hello Your Holiness, I trust you are well."

"As well as can be expected," replied the Pope.

"Well we are all ready for you." Alfred waved his hands across the room, motioning to the cameras.

"Ok Alfred, where do I sit?"

"Right over there Your Holiness, we just need to check the lights."

"I do recall, my dear Alfred, I do recall."

The Pope positioned himself in the red chair trimmed with gold, leaving the Vatican crest in full view above his head. Once settled, Alfred's crew moved in to adjust the light, get readings from the monitors and run a powdered brush over his forehead.

After a few minutes of preparation, Alfred signaled to his crew to leave; he knew the Pope's patience's was running a little thin. He was ready.

"Your Holiness, would you like anything else? Water? Tea?"

"No Alfred, I am ready."

The Pope's words were tinged with a sense of resignation; Alfred picked up on the nuance in his tone. He sensed this would be an important speech.

"Your Holiness, anytime, just let me know when you are about to commence your speech."

"Now Alfred, let's begin."

With that Alfred signaled his control room to begin the countdown.

"Four, three, two and one." Alfred pointed his index finger at the Pope and right on cue the Pope began.

"For everyone listening tonight, I greet you with love and in good faith. I come to you to inform you of some very recent developments that have come to our attention. By now, I am sure you are aware of the situation facing the human race that reaches to every corner of the world. I am speaking of course of MG-J12.

"Throughout history there have been many who claimed to predict the demise of the human race. All have professed to have evangelical information or guidance from God. The Vatican has always reserved comment on these claims.

"Today, we are facing a different situation. After weeks of study, discussion and interpretation of the information that we have acquired, I would like to inform you of the Vatican's position."

He hesitated and took a breath as if to calm himself before he spoke again. "As you are all aware, a theory of the human race's extinction has been circulating, suggesting that our time as inhabitants of God's planet is coming to end. We have heard that God is calling all his children to sit by his side and live forever next to Him.

"In our process of proving or disproving these claims, we have discovered some disturbing revelations. It appears certain that some strains of DNA are indeed changing and these changes will prove fatal. God has decreed that some will live and some will not and we are bound to obey his wishes. Our investigation of the facts has uncovered an anomaly."

He repositioned himself in the chair.

"Our love of God and his son Jesus has sustained us through many a trying time and this time is no different. God has seen our devotion, He has seen our love, He has answered our prayers. Through the miracle of the Lord, we of the Catholic faith have been spared this fate. We have been given a reprieve from God. My brothers and sisters, let us give thanks to the Lord and Jesus Christ his only son. We have been blessed; we have been chosen to be the survivors of this world. We must be grateful for this gift and continue on with our faith. We ask people of all faiths to join us in our quest to honor and love our God and Savior. I pray for all of our children. We are the custodians of this world's future. We will continue to love and serve the Lord with thanks for the great gift He has bestowed upon us.

"As God's messenger on Earth, I welcome all people from around the world to go to our churches, cathedrals or anywhere that can help you convert to our faith. God will accept all; no one will be excluded. The blood and body of Christ is waiting, and I urge you to seek his gift.

"Thank you all. May God be with you."

The camera pulled away from the close up shot and faded to black.

Silence filled the room. No one moved, no one spoke. The only noise was the wheels of the tripod moving across the slate floor.

The Pope stood up from the chair, frail with age, the stress of the situation coming to bear on his tired frame. He stepped down to the floor from the raised TV platform, heading for the exit.

Alfred walked up to him.

"Your Holiness," he said, staring into his eyes. "Are you alright?"

"I am fine my son, just a little tired."

"I understand, Your Holiness. Please let me help you."

Alfred held on to the Pope's arm, guiding him to his entourage. They gathered around, shuffling the Pope in the direction of the doorway and his waiting limousine. As he stepped inside the car they waited for the signal from security to move the procession forward.

The four cars moved in unison as they headed

back to the Vatican. Inside the Pope leaned back into the soft leather seat, gathering his strength for the coming storm.

Chapter 32

June 11th
Washington, DC

"How long have you been standing in line?" said the man in a Washington Capitals jersey to a nervous looking man standing in the long queue in front of the Basilica of the Immaculate Conception.

"I listened to the Pope's speech last night and headed right down here with some food and water. I've been sitting here since. I figured I might as well get in line sooner than later."

"I know what you mean. Can you believe this is happening? I didn't think that I would ever be standing here. I've never even been to church but after watching what's gone on and then that speech last night, there doesn't seem to be much choice."

"I'm with you man, I want to see my children grow up, you know what I mean."

"So where are your kids? Shouldn't you have

them with you?"

"Yep, my ex-wife has them. She was the Catholic in the family, so are all my kids, so I guess it's my turn now."

"A lot of people are thinking that way right now. Good luck man," said the Capitols fan, walking away.

"Yeah you too, aren't you lining up? This is the biggest church in Washington."

"I guess I will. Right now I'm just going to find out how this works."

Within the next two hours the line stretched around the church, then extended for five more miles. The same lines were reported at every church in every state.

Addressing the sudden surge of followers, the Catholic Church outlined the streamlined Rite of Christian Initiation for Adults and published the three page document in every media outlet possible. Becoming Catholic, from start to finish, would now take one month not two years, with virtual baptism available in remote areas.

"As you can see from these live pictures, tonight we have a situation around the planet that speaks to the enormity of the problem. Thousands of people are lining up and turning to the Catholic faith in the hope of escaping the killer gene. Here in Washington, police are struggling to control violent outbursts and incidents of looting as people are reacting to the announcement. If this action continues we will not have to worry about turning Catholic as there are not many people turning the other cheek. I have just been told that tonight, and this is yet to be confirmed, the President will be addressing the people with an update in hopes of controlling these outbreaks.

"This is Jennifer Callwell reporting for NBC news, Washington."

Around the world, chaos ruled as people insisted on instant baptism into the Church. Reports of injured priests trying to defend their churches as they were swarmed by looters in search of any religious relic was a common news story. Gunfire rang out in major cities around the world as pandemonium set in.

Time was running out.

Chapter 33

June 13th
New York City, New York

Surrounded by stacks of papers, Dr. Salter sifted through the data on MG-J12. Pandemic procedures were familiar to him. For the past ten years since assuming his position as head of the World Health Organization he had received hundreds of emails raising the possibility of viruses and diseases invading some place on the planet. In his years of service he had become fully versed with procedures and protocols for handling every situation. Due to sheer volume, sorting real concerns from panic situations took up most of his days. The current most urgent request for his evaluation team was to process the recent viral outbreak on the Caribbean island of St. Lucia.

Months had been spent gathering evidence, verifying and testing samples. Late nights pouring over the information with his team of doctors and virologists had left the team on the verge of a public announcement.

Dr. Salter headed for the boardroom to discuss the strategy of how they were going to handle the worst outbreak in human history.

Dr. Salter was first to arrive in the oversized boardroom. It was not unusual for a group of fifty delegates to travel to this room from around the world. Simon Salter stood at the head of the table leaning on one of the chairs, reviewing his notes. Worry, stress and lack of sleep in the last three weeks had taken a toll on his already thin frame. It became evident to him that morning when dressing as he tightened his trouser belt another notch.

Slowly his team of fifteen arrived, each one armed with morning greetings and their project papers. They randomly selected their place around the boardroom table. Varying in age from the youngest at twenty-five to the oldest at sixty, this handpicked team of biologist, scientists and virologists provided the right balance of enthusiasm and expertise that Simon respected and trusted.

"Firstly, I want to thank all of you for all the hard work you have put in for the last three months. I do understand the sacrifice you and your families have made. I also want to acknowledge that without your dedication and expertise we would not be at this point now. It would have been months before we could have made the announcement I will be giving tomorrow, so your work has saved thousands of lives. Thank you again.

"I think we all know what is facing us as an organization. Each of you has worked on different areas of the MG-J12 sample that came from St. Lucia and I know you have discussed the conclusion amongst yourselves. What I have in front of me is the culmination of our findings that I will make public tomorrow."

He handed over a green, spiral bound, two hundred-page document that made its way around the table.

"The gravity of our findings has prompted me to request a meeting with the President before my announcement. I feel that he needs to understand what the ramifications are for the world's population and to know what our plan is for addressing and eradicating this outbreak. I must tell you," he said, making eye contact with each person around the table, "I am not encouraged by our suggestions or recommendations on how to handle this issue since we have no viable cure or demonstrated origin for this viral outbreak.

"I have a question for the group: do we truly

believe that there is a connection between religious leanings and the mutation of the MG-J12 gene? I find that almost impossible to understand, knowing what we know. It has enormous implication if there is such a connection, so before I conclude, the question again, do we believe that Catholics are immune from this virus while the rest of humanity fights for survival?"

Silence again hung above the heads of the participants like a fog until Dr. Anthony fielded the question.

"Well Simon, as far as I understand and believe, my findings support the immunity of the Catholic faithful to this attack. I believe that to find out why this is happening - or let's say not happening - to them, we would need genetic samples from all the major religions to find out why and right now we do not have that."

"Thanks Stan. I understand your concern, but from the W.H.O.'s position, if we come out tomorrow with a statement confirming this, do you realize what that will do? It will create havoc, if not panic, worldwide. This will be regarded as the end of mankind on Earth. It will rest with us to come up with a cure, a solution or something to stop this, and right now we can't. I am very worried about the fallout."

For the next hour the table discussed their findings and the consequences of the announcement.

"Let me summarize our findings so far," Dr. Salter said attempting to finalize actions. "Our research shows that we have approximately a year between the beginning and its final realization, but we are not completely sure on the time line."

Heads nodded.

"It may be different for each individual but we are confident that within 18 months the full effects are fulfilled. Therefore time is of the essence, to use an overused statement. Every minute saves hundreds of lives.

"That we intend to distribute the antidote as quickly as possible, and we will rely on the agencies that assisted us in other circumstances that have teams of men and woman at the ready to move swiftly in order to get it to as many people as we can.

"It is a monumental task gentlemen, but one that we must undertake. We may fall short in its coverage, but every effort will be made to distribute it to everyone on Earth. The future of the human race depends on this antidote. We must work together to have any hope of survival. In summarizing, we need to help each other, work with each other, and we will live to see our grandchildren smile."

In one unified sign of acceptance, all attendees stood up ready to continue their battle.

Dr. Salter's cell phone vibrated and moved along the table. Excusing himself, he picked up his Blackberry and looked at the unfamiliar number displayed on the screen.

He answered it in a questioning tone. "Hello? Yes, this is Dr. Salter."

After some moments he put his phone back on the table and announced that his meeting with the President was at 10am the next day.

"So gentlemen, it will happen tomorrow at some point after I discuss this with the President. I am sure that once the rest of the world understands what they are facing, we should get ready for lots more work."

Gathering the documentation, Dr. Salter returned to his office to prepare for tomorrow's meeting. He knew it was crucial to communicate to the President the severity of the situation. He had data available to answer every question, except the most important one.

How do we stop MG-J12?

New York City's cacophony of noise was nothing new for Simon Salter. After moving from Hong Kong with his family forty years prior, he had embraced life in Manhattan like a born New Yorker. He enjoyed its attitude and swagger.

He wished he felt more confident this morning. Gazing down on the Hudson from his 14th floor office at the United Nations, he looked at his watch. It was time to head to the main floor to wait for transport to the meeting with the President.

The elevator doors opened immediately and whisked him down to the main floor where he made his way to the front doors. An unassuming brown Crown Victoria pulled up in the parking area in front of the United Nations. A large man got out and headed towards him.

"Dr. Salter?"

"Yes, that's me."

"Could you please follow me?" The man replied without a smile. Opening the back door of the car, he motioned to Dr. Salter to step inside.

"Dr. Salter, my name is Phillip Cross; I will be taking you to meet the President at the Waldorf Astoria. Do you have any questions before we proceed?"

"No, I do not," he replied nervously.

"Ok, then."

They drove across town in silence. Once positioned behind the wheel Phillip pulled out of the semi-circle entrance of the United Nations onto 1st Avenue. Heading north, he drove with meticulous precision, leaving a large enough gap between vehicles to avoid any possible accidents; his Secret Service training remained evident. Turning on East 49th Street, the Crown Victoria blended in with the continual flow of traffic, becoming part of the lifeblood of the streets of Manhattan. Seven blocks after turning onto 49th, Phillip turned onto Park Avenue, steering into the parking area for arriving guests.

"This is where I say goodbye. Someone will be there to take you the rest of the way. Enjoy your day," Phillip said.

"Thank you." Dr. Salter closed the car door. Turning around to enter the Waldorf, he found immediately in front of him another unassuming man ready to continue the escorting procedure.

Once in the hands of the Secret Service there was no chance of varying from the predetermined script.

"Hello, Dr. Salter, I will be escorting you directly

to your meeting with the President and you will have 30 minutes with him. You will remain in front of him at all times. As it has been indicated to us that this is a closed-door session, we will be stationed outside the room. Once you have concluded your business with the President we will escort you to your location of choice. I am sure that the President is looking forward to your meeting. Do you have any questions?"

"No, I think I understood everything," replied Dr. Salter. He was sure that a background check had already been done along with a thorough family history.

"You must understand, not think you understand. If there is anything that was unclear in what I was describing please tell me now."

"No, I understand the protocol, let's proceed," replied Dr. Salter.

"Excellent, then please follow closely behind me, Dr. Salter, and we will make our way up to the Presidential Suite," he said, pointing towards toward the bank of elevators.

The gold art deco doors engraved with classical figures slid open. Entering first, the agent checked out the elevator before Dr. Salter could enter. Welcoming him inside, he waved his security card in front of the reader, clearing the two for the ride up.

"So, Dr. Salter, have you been up to see the President when he has stayed here before?"

"No, I haven't, first time for me."

"Ok, then when we exit the elevator please follow me. The President has the whole floor. You will notice guards at each entrance and exit."

"Certainly, I understand, I will just follow you."

A whoosh could be heard when the door opened, revealing a large hallway which had four doors, two on each side. The agent directed him into one room and pointed to a green high backed chair.

"Wait here and the President will be right out."

Simon felt the true gravity of the meeting weigh on him for the first time.

Suddenly very aware of his posture and his tightly knotted tie, he waited patiently. Looking around the room he noticed the glass topped Eisenhower desk against one wall with space for one chair behind it. The grand piano on the other side of the room reflected the muffled sunlight from its highly polished black top. While taking in all the surroundings, Dr. Salter noticed the far door open. The Secret Service men made their entrance followed by the President, all heading in Simon's direction.

With his hand outstretched the President moved quickly to greet him.

"Good morning Dr. Salter, so nice to see you. I don't believe we have met before."

"Good morning Mr. President. It is an honor to meet you and I want to thank you for your time," Simon said nervously.

"Right then, let's get down to business. I have been briefed on the issue, but I understand that you have additional information that you want to give me."

"Yes, sir. Where would you like me to start?"

"Well, I know a little about MG-J12 because of the recent pandemic alert that your organization issued. I don't know the particulars but I do know that it is making headlines around the world. It has the potential to affect millions of people if we can't find a cure. There is confirmation that it does not affect Catholics, is that correct?"

"Well Mr. President, you are correct on the basics but it has become much more dangerous than anyone ever thought. It appears to be the biggest threat to humanity since the Black Death or the Spanish Flu. In fact we believe it is the greatest problem we have ever faced."

"Do you have a handle on how to control it?"

"Mr. President that is why I requested this meeting. The short answer is that we don't have any control, and we cannot find any way of stopping it. But there is this oddity that you mentioned, that Catholics are immune to it. So far only a few Catholics have died, in comparison to hundreds of others. It is an aberration. They have been completely missed by this MG-J12. We do not understand what is happening. We have never seen anything like this before.

"Let me get to the reason I wanted to talk to you. I would suggest, even plead with you, to reach out to the world to notify them of the severity of the situation. It is imperative that we find a solution if there is one. However in the event that one doesn't exist, it means we are witnessing the demise of the human race as we know it. I am hoping for two outcomes: first, that other scientists around the world will begin to work on this problem immediately, and secondly, that people have time to prepare themselves for the worst."

"Dr. Salter, I hope you realize what you're saying? Are you sure you want to go down that road? If I make an announcement like this you know what the repercussions will be."

"Yes, Mr. President, I think I do, but I see no other avenue right now. We must inform people of what is happening. If we, that is, the World Health Organization, make the announcement, I am afraid that it will fall on deaf ears like the Norwalk or H1N1 did. People are becoming complacent in regards to our notifications. They expect us to be able to find a solution."

"Yes I understand the situation with regard to your organization, but for me to come out and say what you want me to say will create panic and even chaos around the globe. I don't know if I can do such a thing without verifying the seriousness of the situation."

"Mr. President, please feel free to check our conclusions, but I can assure you, we are correct. We have limited time; all efforts have to focus worldwide on defeating this enemy."

"Well Dr. Salter, let me take this issue to the Security Council and I will let you know as soon as I get more information. I will make it a priority."

"Thank you Mr. President. I appreciate your attention and I will wait to hear from you, hopefully very soon," Dr. Salter said.

Turning to leave, Dr. Salter stepped outside the suite doors and waited for directions on when and how to leave the building. He followed the suited Secret Service man out the door back to the elevator bank.

The President picked up the phone as soon as the door closed behind him.

Chapter 34

June 14th
Washington, D.C.

"Thank for joining us tonight on what we feel will be a major announcement from the President. We have three analysts with us to discuss the subject of the speech and who will remain with us throughout the evening to give you a clear understanding of what was said. From left to right we have Bill Collins from the New York Times, Jane Beluce, New York correspondent with the Washington Post, and on the end we have Steven Sinclair from Catholic New York, America's largest Catholic newspaper. Welcome all.

"Before we begin, I just want to tell our audience that we are about 10 minutes away from the President entering the media room at the White House. We will inform you when the President is ready to address the American people. In the meantime, panel, what do you expect from the President tonight? We are all assuming he will address the current situation regarding MG-J12, or as it has been nicknamed 'The Vatican Gene'. Do you have any insight into his handling of the situation? Let me start with Jane Beluce from the Washington Post. Jane?"

"Thank you Ron. First let me say that tonight will be one of those nights in American history that will determine our direction as a nation. Not to scare our viewers but..."

"Excuse me Jane, I have just been informed that the President is entering the media room and is about to begin his address. We will connect to our live feed right now."

The President stood at the podium. Prepared and deliberate he began to speak.

"I am here tonight to share some information with you about the deadly plague that is threatening us. As I am sure you are all aware MG-J12 has invaded our world as it did in prehistoric times. It has had devastating effects. Its far-reaching impact has touched many of us here at home and more families are being affected across the planet. I have been in contact with the World Health Organization and they have assured me that they are working around the clock trying to find a vaccine that will combat this threat.

"But before I continue, a little background may be useful. To those who are skeptical that it even exists, I can tell you conclusively that this latent gene attacks our DNA, modifies it and releases a message to the rest of our cells to shut down our systems. Our bodies no longer protect themselves, our antibodies give up and remain dormant, and by this method MG-J12 is systemically killing all of us one by one.

"As some of you may know, there has been talk of Catholics being immune to MG-J12. Presently there is no proof to confirm such a statement, but we will continue to investigate this claim and I will pass on our findings as soon as we know anything further. I have called a meeting with leaders of the G20 and the United Nations in an effort to share the knowledge we presently have and to coordinate our efforts.

"My fellow Americans, I urge you to take this modern plague very seriously. Understand that it is not contagious - it is a mutation. You do not have to fear your neighbor and there is no magic bullet at this time. However, this is very serious. It is deadly and has to be stopped. We are planning on winning this battle so we can all continue to watch our sons, daughters and grandchildren live in a healthy society. God bless you all. Thank you."

The President stepped away from the podium, speech in hand. He gave the paper to his assistant.

"So, it's done. I tried to be logical, calm and reassuring. Think I accomplished that?" he asked Maria McCauley, the White House Press Secretary.

"I think you did Mr. President. We'll be monitoring the feedback for you."

"Good, thanks Maria. So where am I off to next?"

"Well sir, your next appointment is with your family. We thought you might like some down time with your loved ones. Does that work for you?"

"Absolutely, point me in the right direction."

"Your limousine is waiting."

He leaned into Maria, lightly holding her arm as to get her full attention.

"Thank you Maria. I want you to know that I appreciate your understanding and concern for my well-being. Thank you."

"You are very welcome Mr. President. Enjoy your family time." Maria replied, slightly embarrassed with the attention.

"I will. Believe me, I will."

As he stepped inside the black limousine, the throng of Secret Service men swiveled and turned their backs to the door. Reassured that the President was safely sealed in the car, two taps on the roof signaled to the driver to move out. Slowly moving toward the highway exit its sole passenger closed his eyes in an effort to diffuse the rush of anxiety taking over his thoughts.

Tonight he would spend what hours were left with the people he loved who knew him best and loved him in return.

Chapter 35

June 15th
London, England

"Prime Minister, ready when you are sir…"

"I am ready now, Nigel," the Prime Minister replied.

"3,2,1…" a finger pointed in his direction.

"Good evening. I come to you tonight with an urgent request. As you are probably aware, last night in Washington the President of the United States spoke to his citizens and to the world. His message was an important one. I stand in front of you tonight asking you to take heed of his words. We have faced adversity before. This time it will require a global effort to stamp out this hideous disease.

"So tonight fellow citizens of the United Kingdom, I wanted to reassure you that we are working in partnership with our allies, especially the United States, in eradicating MG-J12. I want to reiterate the President's message and say that we will work to eradicate this disease with all our resources. If we do not, we will share the legacy of the dinosaur and become a footnote of history. This is not a time for international gamesmanship; it is a time for cooperation. England stands ready to take on the challenge."

Already worn out from the constant admittance of patients, the staff at St. Bartholomew's Hospital in London was asked to handle hundreds of calls when the switchboard lit up following the Prime Minister's speech.

The older facility, stretched to capacity, was now dealing with beds in hallways and along unused maintenance corridors. Every corner, space and even closet was used to handle the influx of frightened and ill people. The overworked system needed a break, only none was in sight.

Joan and Glenda, two nurses who had been manning the telephones at the hospital for a week, were making their way back from a coffee run.

"So, what do you make of the Prime Minister's speech?" asked Joan.

"Well, all I know is that we can't handle any more people. What does he expect us to do, build another hospital down the road? I mean, come on," replied Glenda.

"I agree, but this thing is just taking over everything, I am afraid for myself, you know, what if this becomes contagious? It's making me very nervous. Glenda, are you Catholic?"

"Yes I am. I never miss mass, would make me feel too guilty."

"Well I guess you're one of the lucky ones. It's missed you. Maybe I should start going to mass with you, see if it actually makes a difference. Nothing to lose I guess, just my life," joked Joan.

"Well, it's not quite that easy. I've been attending mass since I was a little girl. It's actually quite a procedure to become Catholic, or at least it used to be, and maybe, just maybe, that is why it's not affecting us. Our dedication to God has been thorough and committed. What about if you come with me to my church and I can introduce you to our priest? He will let you know what's involved. I am sure he would be able to help you. I am betting he is a busy man right now; let me talk to him for you."

"I'm going to take you up on that offer; I need to get in touch with my spiritual side. That's what my psychic keeps telling me."

The sound of phones ringing drew their attention away from the conversation.

"Your turn," said Glenda to Joan.

"Hello, St. Bartholomew's Hospital, can I help you?" inquired Joan.

Glenda listened to her co-worker repeat the same message that she had given to the last hundred callers, "Right now sir we have no doctors available. There are no beds and I would suggest you look into another facility that may be able to help you or contact your family doctor. I understand sir, but there is nothing I can do about it. We are all trying to cope the best we know how. Alright, thank you sir, and best of luck."

"Another one looking for the Holy Grail?" said Glenda.

"Yes, I wish I could give them better news, but we are maxed right out. We just can't take one more person."

"Joan, do you think this thing is stoppable? It seems different than the others that we have handled. We have never had the President and the Prime Minister get up there and tell the world how devastating it is. I mean really, do you reckon this could be the end?"

"Come on Glenda, stop talking rubbish. They'll figure it out. Haven't they always figured it out? It's just a matter of time before they find the answer, probably something simple, you know like when they found penicillin on moldy bread," joked Joan, trying to keep her spirits up.

"I sure hope you're right. I need to have some good news soon. There are lots of desperate faces walking through that door," Glenda said, pointing to the line of people pressed against the glass entrance to the lobby.

Chapter 36

"Are you ok Mr. Lynch?" asked Dorothy, tapping at Gordon's office door and stepping inside.

She could tell that Gordon's cough was getting much worse.

"Is there anything I can get for you? Water, some cough syrup, anything?"

"I'm fine," Gordon replied, "I just get these every once in a while. Don't worry, I'm used to it. It's nothing new."

"Ok, Mr. Lynch, but if you need anything, just let me know, won't you?" Dorothy pleaded.

"Yes, I will, don't worry. I'll be fine. Let's get back to work. Do you have that file on the takeover bid that they are trying to force on me, you know, what the hell is that place in Jersey?"

"TechResearch, Mr. Lynch, and it's on the right

side of your desk, just under the blue file folder," Dorothy said as she left the room, closing the door behind her.

She had been with Gordon for as long as he had been in business, watching him move up the ladder in various companies and moving along with him. Although she knew he admired her work ethic and loyalty, she never expected anything from him in return. She knew that it was better that way.

She could hear the coughing continue through the double doors as she sat at her desk just outside his office. It was not getting any better.

"Ok, I understand what the hell you're trying to do, I just don't think that it's a very ethical way to go about your business," Gordon said over the phone to John Abbott, the new head of TechResearch.

"Are you hearing what you're saying Gordon? You of all people talking ethics. Are you fucking kidding me?"

"What? Look at how you're going about this deal. You are trying to take my company right out from under me. You're stealing it!"

"Stealing my ass, you know how it works. I offer more for the shares than the market values them at, your shareholders vote, and you lose. Sounds fair to me."

"Fair, how can that be fair? Somehow you know something that you shouldn't. Has someone been talking to you?" asked Gordon.

"Come on Gordon, secrets are called secrets for a reason. What fun would it be if I told you everything?" laughed Abbott.

"You know you're a son of a bitch, don't you?"

"You and me both my friend, you and me both."

"Hold on a second," Gordon said.

John Abbott listened as Gordon's coughing fit started. It was like a smoker's cough but worse.

"Gordon, Gordon?" he shouted into his speakerphone.

"What? I can hear you," Gordon replied with a gasp. "Ok, I'm back," he said finally. "So where were we? Was the knife fully in my back yet?"

"Not yet, but soon," replied Abbott.

He could hear Gordon coughing again, the sounds tearing from deep inside Gordon's chest.

Gordon sat in his high-backed chair with the phone hanging in his hand. With his free hand he pulled an embroidered white handkerchief from his pocket and placed it in front of his mouth. The rapid fire coughing strained his weakened lungs. His futile effort to stop the hacking only lead to a worse run.

Removing the handkerchief from in front of his mouth he noticed a large clot of mucus splattered with red clinging to the material. Reaching forward again, his body convulsed in an effort to eject the foreign material. He retched uncontrollably and spat out more bloody fluid from his reddened mouth.

"Mr. Lynch! Sir, sir, we have to do something," Dorothy pleaded, running into his office.

Waving her off, he dropped the phone, the receiver hitting the plastic shield under his chair. Trying to speak but unable to breathe, Gordon weakly mouthed the words, "I will be fine."

"No you won't," replied Dorothy, "No you won't, I'm calling an ambulance."

"No, I'll..." another spasm hit him. Bending over in the chair, he threw up a large piece of clotted red phlegm knocking out any air that remained in his lungs. Struggling to replace the air, he winched in pain, gasping.

"Gordon, Gordon!" The voice yelled, swinging back and forth from the wire connected to the phone. "Gordon, are you ok? Come on, answer me!" shouted Abbott.

His coughing continued. Dorothy phoned for the ambulance and ran to get him some water in a hopeless attempt to help.

Gordon slipped down in his chair; his pants rode up his legs, his shirt tightened around his exhausted chest. He fell out of his chair onto the floor, coughing all the while, no longer trying to hold his handkerchief in front of his mouth. Red and pink flotsam covered his white shirt.

Dorothy panicked, desperately looking out the window for the ambulance crew. "Mr. Lynch, Gordon, please, try to sit up, you have to try!"

Looking up from where he lay on the floor, he put his hand on the flat surface of his desk in an effort to right himself, but his arm muscles wouldn't respond to his commands.

Dorothy grabbed both his arms and tried to hoist him upward but he was too big for her to lift. He shifted slightly, trying to help her but fell back again, coughing as he collapsed.

"Hang on Mr. Lynch, they're on their way, they should be here any minute, any minute. Come on, just hang on a little longer," Dorothy said, tears standing in her eyes.

John Abbott could hear everything over the hanging phone line. He listened to Dorothy pleading with Gordon to no avail. He shouted as loudly as he could to get her attention.

Picking up the swaying phone, she asked "What, what do you want me to do, what? You want what? I don't think it is exactly the time for that...Ok, ok." She placed the phone to Gordon's ear.

"Well Gordon, looks like someone got their dues. Did you forget to take your Eucharist today? Don't worry, I'll take good care of the company. May God be with you."

Gordon struggled to respond to John Abbott's statement but the words would not come out. He lurched forward to speak, his eyes bulging. His lungs pushed out a final stream of red as he tried to speak. He looked over at Dorothy and fell back into her outstretched arms, dead.

A minute later the ambulance crew rushed through the door, wheeling the stretcher in anticipation of a rescue.

A half hour later they left the building with Gordon Lynch's body fully covered with a white sheet.

Chapter 37

"I will be retiring for the night," spoke a tired Pope.

"Certainly, Your Holiness, is there anything I can get for you before you retire?" questioned Monsignor Domus.

"No, that will be all, Alberto. I want to thank you for your patience with me. I am feeling my age these days, these many years have worn away at me," smiled the Pope.

"It is always my pleasure, Your Eminence. Have a good sleep tonight and you will feel refreshed by morning," replied Alberto as he slowly closed the heavy door.

Crossing the checkered floor of Italian marble, the Pope headed for the night table next to his bed.

The modest bedroom contained strategically

placed French provincial styled furniture, all made from mahogany, stained with a warm burnt umber color. The five pieces of furniture accompanied by a solitary embroidered cushioned chair worked together to enhance the elegant austerity of the four walls. White sheer curtains with a fine satin backing hung from three oversized windows providing the room with a modest elegance in keeping with the history of the building. The accompanying palette of pastel blues added to its serenity and with the help of a simple wooden cross hanging over the bed, it blessed the surroundings. It was the solitary confinement which the Pope looked forward to every day.

Sitting on the edge of his bed, he removed his brown loafers and placed them neatly next to his bedside table. His blood pressure pills and heart medication were lined up in their orange tinted containers like tiny guardians. Kneeling, he prepared for his nightly ritual.

"I come to You tonight as every night with thankfulness for the day. Today I have witnessed the weakness of man winning out over the trust in Your love and understanding. I grow weary my Father, I am weary of the world. I know You have put this in front of me for a reason, but I cannot see what You want me to see. I pray that You understand my weaknesses. Please heed my prayers tonight. I have been Your faithful servant; You have worked through me all my life. I feel that I have failed you, just now when I need Your consent to continue with what I must do. Forgive me Father. Amen."

Changing into his night clothes, he tugged at the tightly fitted sheets, breaking their hold on his bed. Pulling them back, he raised his legs to meet the linens and he tussled into his favorite position. Mindful of his request, the Pope fought to hear the word of God before he slowly faded into a calming state of sleep.

The ringing church bells sounded in the morning sun. A glow warmed the stones in the piazza as the obelisk's shadow became a giant sundial displaying a seven o'clock wake up call. The procession of delivery trucks unloaded fruits and vegetables and a myriad of delicacies for the morning work of the Vatican chefs. Morning for the papal secretaries was always busily spent preparing for the Pope's scheduled events and meetings. As usual, this day was to begin with a Holy Mass in the Pope's private chapel.

Monsignor Domus hurried down the hallway oblivious to the historical masterpieces hanging on the walls. He had seen them too many times now for them to have any impact. His day always began with a quiet knock at His Holiness's bedroom door.

"Good morning, Your Holiness," Alberto said, tapping lightly on the door. "Breakfast will be served at eight o'clock. There will be time for a mass before then if we head there now," he suggested.

He waited for the door to open or to hear a reply granting his entry into the Pope's quarters. Waiting another minute he knocked again. Silence. Assuming His Holiness was indisposed, he waited a minute longer.

"Excuse me Your Eminence, but may I be of assistance to you this morning?" Alberto waited for a reply.

Nothing.

He knocked again, this time a little stronger and louder, but still there was no sound from inside.

Slowly turning the handle to the unlocked room, he walked in. Remembering His Holiness's words from the previous night he saw his exhausted Pope still asleep in his bed.

"Good morning, Your Holiness," he said, moving forward in the direction of the bed.

"It is time to get up and have some breakfast." He

expected a response by now but there was none. Now standing next to the Pope he shook him lightly so as not to startle the ageing man.

"Your Holiness... Your Holiness," he repeated. "I must insist..." Suddenly Alberto realized what was happening in front of him. He immediately yelled for help, running out of the room desperately shouting for anyone.

He rushed back down the hallway. "Hurry, anyone, please help!" shouted Alberto.

Panic in his face, he ran past people asking them for help and continued running until he reached the meeting of two hallways. Veering to the left his pace quickened and his breathing became more laboured.

"Hurry, hurry," he said as he pushed the door to the medical staff quarters.

"What, Alberto? What is the problem?" asked a resident nurse.

"His Holiness, His Holiness is dying! We must hurry and try to do something, anything, but please hurry," puffed Alberto.

Suddenly the whole room went silent, the shock of Alberto's statement hung in the air as if waiting to fall. The twenty-four hour staff had just done their shift change. They went into immediate action.

"Ok, Alberto, when did this happen?" asked the head nurse Sister Maureen.

"When I went into to assist His Holiness with the morning routine. There was no answer; I knocked twice and then just entered. I found him still asleep in his bed, which was unusual in itself, so I went next to him to wake him and that is when I noticed there was no response at all from him. Hurry, we must do something!" Alberto insisted.

"I will get Dr. Mannicco immediately."

At that instant the whole team moved into the scenario they had trained for. Alarms sounded and the four-man team grabbed medical kits at the ready. Two paramedics and two nurses mobilized in seconds and ran out the room at full speed, Alberto desperately trying to keep up with them.

He heard the emergency call over the overhead speakers.

"Dr. Mannicco, emergency at His Holiness's private quarters, please hurry…"

In three minutes the entire team was at the bedside of the Pope. The wheeled equipment that was pulled along by the team had been set up and hooked up.

The all-in-one monitor registered his vitals, calculating the pulse, heart rate, body temperature and blood pressure of the patient, displaying the verdict to watchful eyes.

Alberto tried to imagine if he could had done something else, what if he had knocked earlier, what if he had entered the first time instead of knocking twice? It was too late now. Grabbing the silver cross that hung around his neck, he knelt down at the end of the bed and prayed. The words "Dear Lord" faintly hit the ears of the medical team as they connected the defibrillator to the chest of the Pope.

"Ready?" questioned Dr. Mannicco.

"Ready," replied the nurse.

"Ok, go," instructed Dr. Mannicco.

Suddenly a jolt of electricity surged through the Pope's body, targeting the heart muscle in an effort to coax it back to work. The monitor showed a flat line with an eerie finality to it, moving along the screen with endless continuity.

"Again," requested Dr. Mannicco.

Another blast hit the lifeless body. Convulsing as if in pain, the Pope's back arched off the bed.

"I am not sure if he can take anymore," said the doctor as he looked at his team.

"He is very weak right now. He may be gone. If we go one more time it could be the last."

"Please, one more time doctor," said Alberto, "Just one more."

Turning his head in the direction of Alberto, Dr. Mannicco's face signaled a sense of hopelessness.

"One more time, please, one more," pleaded Alberto.

Focusing his attention on the lifeless body in front of him, Dr. Mannicco placed the paddles of conductivity over the heart of the Pope. Looking at the nurse his eyes signaled they would go one more time.

"Ready?" asked Dr. Mannicco.

"Ready," she replied.

One more punch was delivered to His Holiness, injecting electricity to his dead heart. It surged again with purpose. The team waited.

"We have a heartbeat! Weak, but we have it!" Dr. Mannicco shouted.

His words transformed the room immediately; the hovering air of despair was changed to one of relief. At the end of the bed Alberto, eyes closed and aimed skyward, put his hands together and spoke two words towards the heavens.

"Thank you." Alberto nodded in gratitude.

"We must get His Holiness to our medical centre as quickly as possible. He will require monitoring for the days ahead and special care. I will make the arrangements immediately."

Grabbing his cell phone he placed a call to the Gemelli Hospital, alerting them to the urgency of the situation. Then he informed the authorities of the need for the Pope's helicopter.

Gemelli Hospital was two and a half miles from the Vatican. With the latest equipment and technology available, it had handled many Vatican emergencies since it was selected as the Vatican's hospital.

"Alright, arrangements have been made. Let's prepare His Eminence for the journey," requested Dr. Mannicco.

"He will be taken by helicopter to Gemelli. They will be prepared as soon as we land so please let's hurry," insisted the doctor.

The monitor's numbers were moving higher as the Pope's body responded to the adrenaline. Dr. Mannicco watched them climb to levels that he was comfortable with before preparing to move the Pope to the helicopter.

Typing on his Blackberry he sent a text outlining the condition of the Pope to the team of doctors waiting at Gemelli. Hitting send Dr. Mannicco glanced at the Pope to reassure himself of his decisions. He noticed the Pope was opening his eyes. Strained by effort his eyelids pushed their way open revealing the brown pupils. Dr. Mannicco quickly crouched down to listen to whatever words were being attempted by His Holiness; his ear was close to the Pope's lips.

"It is time," he mumbled.

"Yes, I know, it is time, we are moving as fast as we can," reassured the doctor.

"It is time," repeated the Pope.

Looking up with greying eyes at Dr. Mannicco, the Pope weakly motioned to his medication that sat on his nightstand.

"Don't worry, Your Holiness, everything is taken care of. We will look after you, your medication will come with us, you will have the best of care," said the Doctor, grabbing the Pope's pills and putting them in his bag.

"We will be flying you to the hospital, everything will be fine. Just stay with us for a bit longer and you will be able to enjoy many more days, Your Holiness, many more days."

Alberto looked from his position at the end of the bed, watching the weakened body of His Holiness struggle to stay with them. He had been with the Pope for over a decade now and knew there was something more to what was happening in front of him.

He moved from the end of the bed to be right next to the Pope. Leaning in the whispered, "Your Holiness, has the Lord spoken?"

Without speaking the Pope slightly moved his head in response to Alberto's question. It was a yes teamed with reassuring eye movement. He returned to the end of the bed, grabbed his rosary and said a prayer with each movement of a bead.

Heading toward the heliport, the Italian police helicopter floated about the Bascilla then passed over the treed garden of the Vatican and landed at the far end of the Vatican grounds. As the rush of air blew the surrounding bushes back, the medical team was protected by the walled waiting area with patient in tow.

"Be careful with how you handle him," said Dr. Mannicco.

"We will doctor, we will," replied the attending doctor waiting inside the chopper.

"We will take it from here, thank you for your help. We will let you know when we have news of his condition," he said, motioning to the pilot to lift off.

"Ok, thank you. May the Lord be with you," were the final words of Dr. Mannicco as the chopper lifted off.

The team watched as it rose above the walled city and pointed its nose down, accelerating in the direction of Gemelli Hospital. All they could do now was wait. Alberto watched and waved goodbye one final time.

Dressed in a blue pin striped suit, Dr. Antionzi sat at a table which contained a myriad of microphones. Surrounded by this team and a Vatican representative, he waited his turn.

First to speak was Father Lombardi.

"I come here today to make known the condition of our beloved spiritual leader, His Holiness Pope John the 23rd. He has endured his health scare and is being cared for by our Vatican doctors. We are hopeful that he will return to resume his position in the near future."

The press scrum continued for half an hour at which time they drew the question and answer session to a close. A few reporters lagged behind in hopes of getting a few more questions in, a favorite trick of the seasoned reporters.

Father Lombardi got up to leave the room.

"Thank you again for your time and information Father Lombardi. I understand the sensitivity of the situation, but before you go can I ask you one more question?"

As the room emptied into the adjacent hallway, Dr. Antionzi headed for the door to a line of six black Mercedes, engines running, doors open at the ready to return everyone to the Vatican.

"Dr. Antionzi," asked the same reporter "Just a quick question."

Dr. Antionzi kept walking to the exit not stopping to acknowledge the question or the reporter.

"Sir, one question, please, just a quick response," cried the reporter.

"I am not stopping, so you better ask me now before I get to the door," replied the doctor.

"Any chance that His Holiness may not fully recover?" questioned the reporter. Stopping immediately after hearing the question, the doctor turned, facing the reporter.

"I cannot comment on that," Dr. Antionzi angrily replied. "That concludes our discussion on this issue. I have no further comment on anything to you."

"Well thank you for your time." The reporter waved as he went out the door with the doctor, one heading one way and the other stepping into a Mercedes.

Chapter 38

June 22nd
Bristol, England

The announcement came through the company's intranet early Tuesday morning.

We are saddened to inform you that our CEO Gordon Lynch passed away Monday morning in Manhattan. After a year of fighting a rare form of lung cancer, he lost his battle. He was the guiding force of GeneQwest, taking the company from its humble beginnings to its current position as the world authority in genetics and molecular biology. He leaves behind his loving wife and two children.

Services will be held at St. Patrick's Church on Sunday April 2nd at 2pm. In lieu of flowers, the family requests donations to the American Cancer Association. Gordon Lynch will be missed by all.

The announcement volleyed around the office

and whispers quickly followed. Sara headed into James' office after reading the announcement.

"So, isn't that something? I figured he had a cold or something when he was here a couple of weeks ago." Sara said.

James looked up from behind his computer screen and replied, "I know, it's surprising how quick these things take hold."

"Kind of scary isn't it? Especially with all the stuff that's happening in the world right now. Maybe it was for the best; he's avoided the inevitable," Sara said.

"Remember what I told you about the whole thing with Gordon and his plan? I hate to say it but it was almost like just desserts, don't you think?"

"I guess so. Still, he was our boss and he did have some good points."

"Really? Can you name one?" questioned James.

"Um, well, he was a father and husband. He still had that going for him."

"I suppose so, I just never saw him as that. The only side I ever saw was the business end, and that wasn't pretty."

Sara noticed James became more uncomfortable as they continued to discuss Gordon's passing. A slight twitch, the frequent repositioning in his chair alarmed Sara that something was bothering James.

"Are you okay?"

"Yes, I'm fine, why are you asking me that?"

"Well, you look weird, kind of sick, and you're sweating when it is pretty cool in here. Are you sure you're good?"

"I will be fine."

"Okay, well you looked like you were about to faint," Sara said.

"No. Guess the announcement of Gordon's death took me back a bit, that's all"

"That's understandable; you worked with him the most."

James paused, considering his next step. He could feel the sweat building on his forehead. His mouth was dry and he felt a pounding headache coming on.

"Sara, there is something I think you should know."

"I hate it when someone starts with those words. Before you start, do I really need to know?"

"I don't know if you *really* need to know, but I need to tell someone."

"James, what the hell are you talking about?"

"Well, after I had that discussion with Gordon, the one I told you about, I decided that something had to be done - something that probably only I could do."

"Do you mean discovering a way to stop this mutant gene?

"No, something else."

"Ok, James, let's stop this guessing game. Would you just tell me what you're talking about?"

"I killed Gordon."

"You what?" she cried. Realizing her words could be heard around the office, she lowered her volume. "You killed Gordon? That's impossible. He died in New York. You were with me last night, remember?" Sara felt her pulse quicken.

"I remember."

"Then what the hell are you saying about killing Gordon?" she said, her voice now a whisper.

"You know the medication that he was on, the one that both you and I worked on for the cancer research project? Well, I adjusted a few things in it."

"James – that serum was purely experimental. What 'few things' did you adjust?"

"I introduced some isotopes, increased them slightly each time he asked for a new supply. I just couldn't watch him do what he was doing..." James said helplessly. "In the end I upped the amount to a lethal dose."

"James." Sara looked puzzled. "It's not like you to do such a thing. How could you do it? You know that's murder. I don't know what to think right now," she said, raising her hands in frustration.

"I know Sara, that's why I warned you before that if I told you it would involve you or lead to something you don't want to be associated with." James couldn't look at her directly. His eyes scanned everywhere looking for some object to focus on, and his guilt was obvious to Sara.

"James, I know you are an ethical person, I know you are a kind person, you are someone who weighs each and every action. Killing someone is not what I had you down for. How am I supposed to react to something like this?"

"Believe me Sara, it has weighed heavily on me since I started Gordon on that path, but I couldn't see how I could let the world be his plaything. We are talking millions of lives; we are talking controlling the Vatican. Do you know where that put him? It made him the most powerful man on the planet and he was using all of us for his own personal gain. It was wrong and I couldn't let it continue. Am I making any sense?"

"Yes and no. I can see your motivation for doing it. I understand your logic and reasoning but wasn't there any other course of action you could have taken?"

"I couldn't see one."

"Maybe you should have looked a little deeper," Sara replied.

No immediate answer came to James' mind; his worried expression betrayed the fact that he thought he had just made a terrible mistake in telling Sara everything.

"Sara, I cannot go back and change things, and to tell you the truth I don't know if I would. Gordon is gone; I doubt that there will be an autopsy, so this could remain between you and me. I can't think of anything else to tell you, if sorry helps, I'm sorry. I know you didn't think I was that type of person."

"Well you're right on that last point, James. I don't know what to tell you. I have to think about this."

"I understand," James replied, looking directly into her eyes.

Sara quickly weighted up her options. Timing was everything. James's confession had fallen into her lap unexpectedly. It would all nicely fit together now with one text message.

Chapter 39

June 24th

Bristol's chilly, ocean-scented night air blew around James as he slid the key into the tarnished lock and pushed the door open. Illumina stood in darkness. Prior to reaching for the light switch he snatched a deep breath, carrying inside as much ocean air as his lungs could hold. It rejuvenated his thoughts.

Once a beehive of activity, now stillness greeted him in the lab. Gordon's passing had left the lab in limbo: all research halted, no one knew what would be the next step. James informed his team that for the interim there would be nothing to do until the board in New York decided what direction to take. The first matter of business was to replace Gordon so work at the lab was suspended until further notice.

Soft lighting from the limited lights James had switched on imparted an eerie glow to the lab. He walked around scanning each desk as he passed. Scattered papers, pictures of children, wives and dogs hung from walls or cubicles. His circle tour stopped at Sara's office. He pushed the almost closed door open. Concerned he was invading her sanctum, he cautiously walked further into her office. Looking around he got a sense of what was important to her. Pictures of her pub friends, a small United States flag standing at attention and her framed certificate from Berkeley stood out first. Leaning against a stack of reference books in her bookcase James noticed a small picture frame. The three-by-five black frame faced Sara's chair. James advanced to the other side of the desk to get a clear look. An elderly man stared back, possibly in his seventies, distinguished and poised. He had never seen it before.

Headed back to the close up for one last time, Coldplay's 'Every Teardrop' punctured the silence. The chorus was set as the ring tone on James's cell phone.

"Hello?"

"Hello James, this is John Abbott. I don't believe we have ever met."

"I think you have the wrong number."

"I don't think so. You're James Mitchell of Illumina Labs?"

"Yes, that's me."

"Ok, I have the right person. James, let's start again."

"What is the reason for your call?"

"I understand you are the person in charge of Illumina Labs?"

"Yes." James's confusion prevented him from using too many words.

"I wanted to call you personally before the news got out to let you know that I am the new CEO of GeneQwest."

James hesitated, surprised by this information. "Well… thank you for the call."

"I'm sitting here in New York and thought that you and I could get together to chat about things. Let's say next week? I will come to Bristol and we can work some issues out."

"Alright, we can meet, but I'm not sure what there is to discuss."

"Well, let's just say that I might have a proposition for you."

"What might that be Mr. Abbott?"

A longer than normal pause hung between the two.

James jumped in first. "I'm not sure what you

know about Illumina and its work?"

John quickly interjected, "James, I know everything, even beyond what you know. That is why I would like to discuss the options that we both have."

Puzzled by the answer James's face unconsciously contorted.

John continued. "We will get to that when I am there. I will be in touch regarding timing. Until then hang tight."

James said nothing.

"Thanks James, talk to you soon."

James pocketed his phone, replaying the conversation in his head he walked out of the lab and back into the cool Bristol night.

Chapter 40

The opening notes of the BBC news reached James's ears as he sat down to eat breakfast.

"Good morning. This is the BBC morning news and I'm Alan King. For our opening story this morning we have with us Dr. Cameron Kershaw from the Academy in Rome. Thank you very much for joining us this morning."

"You're welcome Alan."

"Dr. Kershaw, can you give our viewers an update on the status of your work? I understand that it has now expanded to include a multitude of scientists and geneticists around the world. Are you seeing any progress?"

"That is correct; we have been battling this mutation for three months now with little to no results, so we have put together this team via the Internet to increase our capabilities and to collaborate and correlate our findings."

"I would like to say we are making progress, but we are dealing with an extremely complex problem. The variations on possible combinations are over 3 billion."

"Do you have any sense of when you will have what is considered a breakthrough?"

"Regrettably I don't. We have the best in the world working on it and I do believe we will find the answer. I just cannot tell you when."

"What do you consider the main stumbling block?"

"Nature."

"Can you explain that to our audience?"

"I'll try. Nature has locked its secrets up in a sort of cryptic sequence. Its coding requires multiple progressions to get to the next level. In simple terms, it would be like having one door to open but you have to try billions of keys to open it. We need that one key, that one clue to open the door that will guide us to what we need to understand."

"That helps to explain to all of us the magnitude of the task, thank you. I am sure that when you do find the combination we will certainly hear about it. Dr. Kershaw, I want to thank you for joining us this morning, and though we had hoped to hear more encouraging news, we will leave you to the task at hand."

"You're welcome Alan."

"Thank you again, Dr. Kershaw."

The camera zoomed in, capturing the reporter's face in anticipation of his sombre remarks. "Well there you have it. It seems we are no closer to finding the key to our survival. We must continue to place our trust in science.

"For BBC London in the Morning this is Alan King."

In synchronization with his words a stock picture of the Vatican scientists flashed on the screen.

James stiffened as he watched the interview. The reporter's words sunk into his brain like quicksand.

Pacing up and down the wooden hallway between his bedroom and kitchen, James heard his slippers drag on the floor. Back and forth down the same path. He knew he needed a plan, a method to get the antidote to the world without implication. Logical thinking was his strength; nothing rash, no quick decisions. Rubbing his forehead he walked back down the hallway.

James glanced at the hallway mirror in passing and was startled at the sight of his reflection. He barely recognized the eyes he had inherited from his mother and his father's stoic features. Fatigue from the stress of the last few months had etched deep lines on his face. He pulled his hands down, slowly stretching the skin. Staring at himself he knew something had to be done. Time was running out. He played back the recent events.

He had corroborated in the manipulation of the Vatican. Gordon was dead. He worked on the tissue, the clue. Only Sara knew about Gordon and how he died. Gordon must have set up something with a church official but they would never tell anyone what they did.

Suddenly he remembered Heather in the lineup with of the Vatican recruits. He had the key, the antidote. Heather was the answer.

Chapter 41

June 26th
Rome, Italy

British Airways Flight 68 touched down at Leonardo da Vinci Airport, International Arrivals, Terminal B. The clicking of unbuckled seatbelts heralded the anticipated rush of exiting travelers. Humid air flowed into the cigar shaped cylinder as the cabin door opened.

James followed the queue into the airport's greeting area. Large white metal trusses spanned the enormous baggage area bouncing back the Italian, French and English announcements. Ten minutes later he stood outside looking for transportation to the predetermined meeting place.

Two weeks earlier James had designed the email subject line to catch Heather's attention: *Solution in hand.*

Heather,

It's James Mitchell. I'm not sure if you remember me, but we worked together for a semester back in Cambridge seven years ago. We spent many a night discussing a myriad of problems that we were engaged in. I saw you on television a few days ago and wanted to touch base with you. I know you are working on solving **the** *problem and I have some information that might be beneficial to you. I don't want to discuss it over the phone or email. How about we meet? Let me know your schedule and I will work around you.*

Best, James.

The half hour cab ride from the airport afforded James a quick tour of Rome. Its ancient ruins stood among the modern architecture as if challenging them to match their longevity. The relentless flow of traffic raced along with choreographed precision. James gripped the door handle in anticipation of a collision.

Stopping in front of a rundown building, the driver turned and used the internationally understood thumbs up indicating they had arrived at James' destination.

Il Simposio was a small coffee bar frequented by locals and located far from the usual thoroughfares. Its venerable appearance demonstrated it had been through many transformations during its existence.

Stepping out of the taxi, James immediately spotted Heather sitting outside at one of the small round tables crammed into the corner of Il Simposio's limited outdoor space. Threading through tables, James stood in front of Heather waiting for her to notice him.

Heather stood up and immediately spread her arms in a welcoming hug.

"James! It's so nice to see you after, what is it, seven years?"

"About that. You look great, haven't changed a bit."

"Oh, come on James, you're just being polite."

"No, really, you look great."

"Ok, I'll take that," smiled Heather. "Come sit down," she said, motioning to the empty chair. "Let me order something for you. How about I order you some coffee? Italians do it differently you know. Plus I have a thing for coffee."

"Ok, I won't question that, go ahead and order something for me."

Heather waved at the roving waiter and told him what James would have. The waiter nodded and dodged through the tightly packed tables.

"So, I was surprised to see an email from you.

After I left Cambridge we lost contact. I figured it was just one of those things that happens, you know?"

"For sure, chalk it up to a university friendship right? You go one way and I another, but then I saw that group shot at the Academy and recognized you. I figured I had to make contact - you were a superstar."

"Little generous with that one, James. I'm just part of the team trying to solve this predicament." Heather couldn't help smiling at the compliment though.

"Doesn't seem to have affected many people here," James said, looking around the packed coffee house.

"They're Catholic. Italy has the largest Catholic population in Europe."

"Right. And it misses them."

"Apparently it does," Heather said.

James's coffee was deposited in front of him. The black solution stood out against the white porcelain mug.

"Go on, taste it," urged Heather.

"I will, just need to put a few things in it. Where's the cream and sugar?"

"James, you can't do that! You'll lose the true taste of the coffee."

"I'm sure I will, but can't drink it otherwise," he

smiled as he added his required mixture from the containers on the table.

Sipping the hot liquid he sampled the strong roast blend. "Very good - different than what I'm used to, but very tasty."

Smiling at James, Heather raised her eyebrows.

"No really, it is, I like it."

"Ok, good, I was wondering there for a minute."

Heather pulled her chair closer to the wooden table.

"I presumed from your email there was more you wanted to talk to me about?"

James was quickly reminded of Heather's direct manner.

"I wanted to talk to you about some developments I've been working on. I thought they would be of interest to you, especially after I saw your new position."

"So what is it?"

Surveying the other people in the coffee bar, James repositioned his chair closer to Heather and nervously launched into his explanation.

"I want to let you tell you something but I have to have your assurance that it will stay with you. And I mean only you."

"What are you talking about, James?" Heather said loudly.

Indicating for her to lower her voice, James said, "I just need your assurance at this point."

"I guess I have to say okay, but it sounds rather daunting."

"Well it is, but in a good way."

"Fine, let's hear this secret."

"I know you don't like long drawn out set-ups, so here it is. I have found the solution to the world's problem; I have an antidote that will stop this mutant gene from killing us."

His delivery was matter of fact and caught Heather off guard. She remained speechless for a moment, her eyes wide open. Finally she replied. "Do you mean that we are busting our butts trying to find the answer, and you've already solved it?"

"Yes," James replied quietly, scanning the surroundings.

"And you're keeping it from the rest of the world for what reason?" Heather replied, raising her voice. "I don't know what to say, James, I wasn't expecting that. I thought maybe there was some new project or company you wanted to discuss with me, but never, and I mean never, something like this. Really, James? Am I missing something here? Why don't you announce it, take the credit and save the world?" Heather said.

"You are missing some crucial information that I can't give you and that's the reason you can't say anything. It's very complicated. I've gotten myself into a position I can't easily get out of. There are certain parties that would have some... let's say feedback, to my releasing the information. I thought you could help."

"So you want me to take your findings, release them and not mention you at all?"

"That's right."

"You know that the Academy will end up taking credit. You're alright with that?"

"Absolutely. My goal is to get this antidote to the world. I don't care who gets the credit. I am past all that stuff."

"And how do you propose that I suddenly come across this discovery? You know it has to have back up and testing?"

"I have everything you need and more. I know it works, in fact it is working as we speak."

Heather scrunched up her face into a penetrating

stare.

"I know it doesn't make sense but you have to look past that. We just need to get this to everyone. Once that happens others will see results and we can continue living. We're under attack by Mother Nature; you've seen the results and the pattern."

"Yes I have, and that is why the Academy put this team together. We have some of the greatest scientists in the world."

"I'm betting you are the youngest of the lot?"

"Yes I am, but how is that an advantage?"

"You have fresh ideas, new approaches; you are not stuck in traditional methods. That's the angle."

"So let's say I do go along with this: I announce to the team that I have discovered the answer. Then what?"

"From there the World Health Organization, the CDC and every other organization will step in and get it to the world. They did it before with bird flu. They won't get it to everyone in time but it will stop the devastation. It'll be a new beginning."

"How long does your antidote take to modify the DNA?"

"Almost immediately. It modifies the RNA and amino acids and it attacks the mutant gene and nullified its affects."

"So tell me James, do I need to know more about why you can't step forward with this yourself?"

"I could tell you if you want but it would be not in your best interest."

"And you know that for a fact?"

"I do. Trust me - you don't want them interested in you."

"Well, you have successfully scared me off. I guess I'll just let sleeping dogs lie."

"That would be best."

"So how do you propose to get the information to me? Is it written down or hidden somewhere?"

"No, I have it right here on a flash drive. It is in my pocket. Once I pass it to you, you'll be able to take it from there. I know you'll understand the principles and put it in your own words." James reached into his pocket and passed her the red flash drive.

"This is it?" asked Heather.

"That's it." James nodded. "There is a lot of information on there. I've included all the documents you need to defend the discovery. It's all there."

Heather peered around to see if anyone was watching. She put the flash drive in her leather purse, zipped it shut and held it close to her body.

"Keeping it secure?" asked James.

"I'm making sure it doesn't fall out when I get on my scooter. We don't want it getting into the wrong hands do we?"

"I think it's a little too late for that."

"Too late? Are you saying someone already has this information?"

"Sort of?" James replied, regretting his previous statement.

"Sort of? What does that mean? They're either using it or there're not."

"You could say a bit of both."

"You're confusing me...?"

"Sleeping dogs, remember?"

Heather nodded in acknowledgement. "Is there anything I should know about what's on the flash drive? Steps or procedures I have to follow?"

"It's all laid out in the files. This is all yours from this point on. You'll be in the spotlight. Are you sure you're ready for this?"

"I'll be fine. I've had a few discoveries in my day," she said, grinning.

"I know. I've done some research on your

findings. They're very interesting. I guess that's why you were picked to be on the Vatican's team."

"I guess so. This will blow all of them out of the water. For all of our inspired conversations back in Cambridge I never did ask you James: are you the religious type?"

"No, I'm afraid I'm not, too many years of research."

"You've never thought about where your passion for the sciences came from?"

"Not really. Where are you going with this Heather?"

"Just asking, that's all. You've never thought about your lifework or calling in the sciences as a way God is working through you? Your discovery will save us, save millions of people. Perhaps there's a chance that God selected you from all of us to be the one that finds the solution?"

"I really don't think so." James appeared anxious with the line of questioning.

"I have wavered over the years," Heather said, spinning her spoon in her coffee. "I look at what we do as scientists as discovering entities or mechanisms that are already in front of us. We are not finding out anything new, we are just rediscovering the unknown. Have you ever thought about who put it there in the first place? From the big bang to now, it's just there. I know it all sounds a little over the top, but I have a trust in evidence and a logical, provable approach to research. But what does that prove? Maybe God is like a puzzle, you have to put the pieces together to find the answer. That's why I joined the Academy; I believe there's a connection between religion and science, a partnership of sorts. They can work separately but when put together they form a partnership, a collaboration for humanity."

"That's quite the statement. I really hadn't thought of it like that, not sure I ever will."

"I have. After years of research and questioning, I began to look at things with a different point of view, one of belief instead of skepticism. Sorry, getting a little philosophical on you."

"A little?"

"Ok, I know when I've said too much." Heather smiled.

"Not really. It's an interesting interpretation of what we do, but one query I have is, what question are you trying to answer?"

"I'm not sure yet, but I will know when I find it."

"I'm sure you will. Until then I look forward to seeing you on the TV as part of that successful team announcing the cure."

"I'll be there in the front row," Heather laughed.

Standing up and preparing to leave the coffee bar, both realized that it would a long time before they met again.

"Almost forgot, thank you for handing me the limelight. I am sure you knew what this would do for me in the science world, it's much appreciated." She moved in closer and gently planted an innocent kiss on his cheek. "Goodbye James. What else can I say, really, except that I will be thinking of you on the day."

"And I of you. I'm sure we will see each other someday soon. Take care Heather and God speed." James smiled.

James watched Heather's yellow scooter duck between the traffic until it disappeared.

Chapter 42

Heather's yellow scooter zipped in between the colorful lines of compressed traffic becoming part of the daily Roman opera of orchestral honks and manic hand gestures. She drove with precision, carving through the congestion to arrive at work unscathed.

The fifteen minutes on Rome's roads boosted her adrenaline better than her beloved espresso ever could. Joining other scooters parked in their designated area, Heather removed her matching yellow helmet, adjusted her knapsack and took in the fresh morning air before heading into the Academy for the start of another day.

A few people were already sitting at their computers deciphering the overnight reports, trying to find the one needle in their DNA haystack. Four weeks on from their first meeting with Cameron, the group was still coming up empty handed. Disappointment and exhaustion surfaced on their faces from time to time.

The heavy concentration impacted their ability to think clearly and breaks were mandated to pull them away from the ever-changing iterations of the DNA model.

Today's break was a short meeting with Cameron in the common room.

Helmet in hand, Heather walked past some earlier arrivals. "Morning all," she said, blanketing three or four people with her salutation.

"Morning," was echoed back, though most did not raise their eyes from the screen. It was a normal morning and Heather didn't expect much more.

Sitting down at her desk, she wondered if this would be the day they were waiting for. It was the same question she had asked herself every morning since the mission began.

Around 10 a.m., the team trickled in and took over the common room chairs. Cameron leaned against the kitchen counter and began the meeting.

"Good morning everyone, thanks for taking the time. I just wanted to gather everyone today to discuss, engage, talk - whatever word we want to put in there - to find out how everyone is handling the situation. I know that it has become a frustrating task and results are hard to come by, so I just want to let you know a few things.

"First, I am sure you are all aware that things are getting worse; the death toll is rising, except for Catholics, of course, which brings me to the reason for this short interlude. The movement to Catholicism by, let's say, a highly motivated population, is creating an issue, both for the Church and for the other faiths that are being abandoned. The rules around baptism are being reexamined. I believe that in the short term there will be an announcement of a type of modification, from my limited information it appears the whole process will now take three weeks, but I understand the Vatican is addressing this as we speak.

"How does this apply to your work? Well, short term, the focus of the team will be on the samples from non-Catholics that have not been affected. This is a shift in our direction as our first mandate was to look into the DNA of Catholics to see why they have been excluded from this epidemic. The focus now will be on the growing samples that are coming in from people who are not Catholic but have no indication of mutant gene growth."

Clapping his hands together Cameron continued, "I have said enough, you will receive an email shortly to notify you of our new direction. Thank you again for all of your efforts."

"Oh, also, just before you go, I wanted to let you know that I have sent an email to everyone reminding us about our mission here. It's a quote from Pope John to help us to remember why we seek answers. That's all I have," said Cameron.

As she listened to Cameron's upbeat delivery, Heather noticed several people fidgeting and looking around the room while he spoke. For them his approach was wearing thin and his motivational speaker style was unnecessary. For others it was the kick they needed to spur them on. Heather sided with the latter.

Returning to her office, she saw Cameron's email in the corner of her computer screen waiting to be opened. Heather clicked on the icon and it opened in full screen mode to display the words of Pope John.

Cameron's subject line read: *Words to Remember – Our work at the Vatican Academy.*

"Nature is a book whose writing and meaning we decipher with the sciences, while remembering the presence of the author who wishes to reveal himself within it."

Heather read it again while chewing the end of an

already worn blue pen, absorbing the words.

Her thoughts turned to the flash drive stored in her knapsack. It was too early to announce her findings; she needed to become familiar with James's research and his procedural sequence. Understanding the questions that were going to be aimed her way after her announcement, her knowledge of the subject matter and all that had gone before would be beneficial. The coming weekend would be perfect timing to review James's research and findings and go through her stack of *Science* magazines. She had kept every issue since becoming a subscriber and they were part of her boxed treasures when she moved to Rome; now they were all neatly stacked in the bookshelf at her apartment. She knew what she would be doing for the next couple of days.

As dusk approached, its warm glow transformed the biscuit colored buildings into a sepia collage of ancient postcards. As Heather headed for home, perched on her yellow scooter, the cacophony of traffic noise seemed far away. She was replaying the last line in Cameron's email, 'the author who wishes to reveal himself within it.'

Turning the ancient key in the well-worn lock she

pushed the door inward. Her one bedroom apartment on the third floor was considered small even by Roman standards. Compact in design, it had been her home and her own little world since she moved from Dublin. Austere furniture made of wood with colourful cotton cushions sat in the middle of the floor. Her only indulgence in the unadorned kitchen was a Gaggia coffee machine, a restaurant model, that sat on the kitchen counter like a hunting trophy.

Hanging her helmet on the oversized hook, Heather hurried to her laptop. With one press on the keyboard the familiar chorus of Windows 8 startup signaled the software was agreeable. Inserting the flash drive into the USB port, it automatically began the handover process and her Friday night.

The dialogue box suggested it needed 3 minutes to complete the download. Plenty of time for Heather to kick start her coffee machine. A perennial Italian coffee favorite, Lavazza dark roast was the only coffee in her kitchen. The pungent aroma immediately filled her small apartment penetrating everything; a subtle four beat chime signified her pot of caffeine was ready.

Balancing her black coffee and laptop, Heather headed for the couch, prepared to absorb all of James's research. Her weekend would be spent indoors doing homework.

Saturday morning began the same way Friday ended, interpreting James' information, absorbing his methodical footsteps and understanding his final analysis. Sunday night would arrive too quickly. As she reviewed the material James had sent her, she realized that it was almost completely outside the areas that the Vatican group had been exploring. She would need something to justify her new direction of inquiry.

Heading to her floor to ceiling bookshelf she pulled out a stack of magazines, looking for articles that would build her case and confidence. One after another, she first skimmed the covers of the magazines and then thumbed through the index in hopes of recognizing articles that pertained to her needed subject matter. Neatly restacking the ones that were of no use to her she ploughed through the rest of them. Her pile of worthwhile reading grew to almost the size of her discarded one. Heather's pace quickened as she neared the end of the pile and her endurance.

Repositioning herself on one side of the small couch, she started the process again, issue by issue refining her research. The night air leaked into Heather's apartment, hinting at the lateness of the evening as the pile by her side rose up to her knees. She had gone through over one hundred editions of the magazine. Picking up another issue, she promised herself just ten more minutes before she would break for a late evening snack.

With a sigh of relief, she straightened her back against the sofa. She became aware of the aroma of the coffee she had put on numerous times during her investigation as it floated on the breeze of the night air. Confident that she had read enough, her passion for java got the best of her and she got up to make herself a cup.

Returning, she opened the magazine to the page where an article began. Delving into the article, she read how the gene A02379, a heritable gene, altered monoamine levels to create a possible DNA restriction. It continued on to describe test results that showed natural selection could play a role in DNA structure. Could that change have accelerated as a result of exposure to the Vatican Gene? Was MG-J12 the evolutionary warrior gene that James found, programmed to act when threatened?

Heather finished the article and put down the

magazine. Coffee in hand, she stood up and headed for the twin windows, looking out pensively on to the street below. She ran the scenario through her mind, quickly processing the mathematical runs she would do tomorrow at her computer.

Tomorrow would be the acid test; right now she needed to rest, eat something and get a good night's sleep.

Morning came quickly. Sunlight broke through the only crack left between two adjoining curtains and took direct aim at Heather's eyes, warning her to wake up. Throwing on yesterday's jeans and a clean white blouse, she grabbed her helmet and made her way down the stairs to her parked scooter.

Six in the morning was still quiet for Rome and Heather zipped through the streets as though it was a racecourse. In record time she arrived at the Academy and sprinted up the two flights of stairs to her office. She hit the mouse, activating the machine's request for her password, as she threw her light jacket over the back of a chair.

Mindful of the test requirements, Heather picked a DNA sample, noted its donor's origin and confirmed that they were a victim of the mutant gene. The donor was a Buddhist. Seconds later the electron microscope scanned the sample and displayed the results of her selection.

Next she requested another sample to compare the DNA and molecular makeup. She chose a sample noted as an infected Protestant. Displayed together, the answer spun in front of her with clarity. The mutant gene had run rampant through both. The MG-J12's deadly amino acids attach themselves to the proteins, which in turn infected their DNA. God was in the details and those details were displayed to Heather in no uncertain terms.

Time to introduce James's antidote.

Heather leaned back, slightly slumped in her chair, hands on the back of her head for support. She watched the helix model turn slowly and with each turn it displayed its complex beauty, crafted by James from a scrap of ancient tissue and a questioning mind.

The rest of the team began funneling into the lab, each heading for their desks in preparation for another day of battle. Heather barely registered their arrival. Without reservation and walking with confidence, she headed directly to Cameron's office. Standing tall, she knocked and entered his office.

"Morning Cameron, do you have a few minutes to discuss something?" Heather asked.

"Sure, take a seat. What can I help you with this lovely morning, Heather?" smiled Cameron.

"Well, it's not really help I need. I'll get right to the point. I believe I have found it, and by 'it' I mean a cure," Heather said, "I believe I have… in fact I know I have. I have seen it with my own eyes. All the tests I've run show the same result, there is no doubt. This is it."

"Heather, that's wonderful! Wait, there has to be a better word - that's fantastic, marvelous, spectacular. Choose anyone one of them, what I mean is congratulations." Cameron beamed. "You know, of course, that we have to rerun your results before we release anything. I'll get the team on it right away." He turned around, not sure who to call first. Heather started towards the door.

"Just before you go," Cameron said, his hand already holding his phone, "Remember our original conditions, this has to remain the project's announcement. Please don't talk to anyone in the media whatsoever, understood?"

"Perfect, I'll leave that up to you. I don't want any part of it. I am just glad we've finally solved this."

"So am I," said Cameron, "So am I."

Cameron gathered the team immediately. When the announcement was made the round of applause caused Heather to blush as one by one the other scientists shook her hand and offered their congratulations. She recalled the words of James at the coffee bar, "Can you handle the attention?"

Cameron instructed them to verify Heather's results using different sets of parameters.

After 48 frantic hours of round-the-clock retesting, it was confirmed that Heather's discovery was correct. It was time to release the news to the world. With the results tucked under his left arm, Cameron walked back to his office from the print room, closed the door behind him and picked up his Blackberry. Scrolling through his contacts, he pressed call.

"Good Morning, Your Holiness," Cameron said. "I have good news. It is done, the discovery has been made." In a whisper, Cameron quickly outlined the results of Heather's research.

"Thank you Cameron, you have done a great service to us all. I will handle it from here."

As he shut off his phone, the Pope looked skyward and whispered, "Thank you Lord for answering my prayers. Now I know what to do." The Pope returned to his office and immediately called Alberto.

Cameron listened to the signal fade as he moved the phone farther from his ear. His duty was done, the weight was lifted from his shoulders and now he was just one of the millions who would wait to see God's will be done.

Chapter 43

The medical team in charge of the Pope's recovery was on twenty-four hour watch. His slow but successful return to health, tracked by the Italian dailies, was reported as further evidence of God's hand at work. The Pope's release from hospital was anticipated within the week.

While resting in his hospital bed the Pope watched television to keep abreast of the world's view of the latest efforts to combat the mutant gene. Lines still formed outside Catholic Churches as people waited to become one with his faith. Catholics still remained immune. He began to wonder if something else was at play.

Pressing the red button connected to his room, the Pope called for the nurse.

"Yes Your Holiness, is there something I can get

for you?"

"Yes, I would like you to ask Cardinal Gagnon to come and see me."

"Right away, Your Holiness."

"Thank you."

The nurse dutifully followed up with the Pope's request and within one hour Cardinal Gagnon was standing at the end of the Pope's bed.

"I am at your service, Your Eminence."

"Cardinal Gagnon, it is nice to see you."

"It is even better for me to see you," smiled the Cardinal. "We need you to lead us through these times. I am thankful."

"That is very kind of you, Cardinal, but I have asked you here for a reason, I need to discuss something that I hope you can help me with."

"Absolutely, Your Holiness."

Propping himself up on his bed, the Pope started with one question. "Cardinal Gagnon, is there something I should know about what is happening at the Vatican?"

"I am not sure what you mean, Your Holiness."

"Did Gordon Lynch's proposal get implemented?"

Cardinal Gagnon's face reddened and his eyes

wandered around the room.

The Pope knew the answer before Cardinal Gagnon could utter one word.

"Your Holiness, I cannot continue with this situation. It has weighed heavy on my heart since it was first proposed. There was a group that has moved in another direction from the one you had chosen. I am not sure who they all are as I have not participated in any of their decisions or actions, but I do know that Cardinal Hickey is the organizer of this initiative."

"Thank you Cardinal Gagnon." As the Pope lowered his eyes, his heartbeat monitor beeped at an increased pace. "I appreciate your honesty, but why did you not come to me when this was happening?"

"I do not know why, Your Holiness, only that I hoped that would it would not have been agreed on by others. That it would have failed in the planning."

His confession was received in silence. Recognizing that there was nothing else to say, the Cardinal turned away from the Pope's bedside and left the hospital room.

Chapter 44

Pope John's return to the Vatican was heralded as miraculous and his weeks of recuperation had given him time to mull over his approach to the mutiny.

The bells rang out in St. Peter's Square in honour of the Pope's return. The usual crowds of tourists and locals had thinned to a few dozen as people kept to their homes in fear. More deaths were reported each day to the despair of the remaining authorities in every country. Empty streets, unused roadways, and grounded aircraft testified to the scope of the tragedy. Depression crept around the planet like a snake. It slithered into the heart of every family, stirring darkness into the soul of mankind.

Slowly pacing back and forth in his office, with lowered head and hands folded in prayer, Pope John walked the worn grey slate floor. Without his vestments, he looked less like a Pope and more like the ordinary man he felt he had become. His prayers were not being answered. He had considered what they had done; he considered what the Church had done. The swelling numbers of new believers and returning agnostics had created a rush to confirmation. The daily lines continued to grow at churches and cathedrals around the world. Hope had been funneled into a single option and the edicts from various denominations faded to nothing as desperate people took the road to survival through Catholicism.

A gentle knock at the door as it edged open indicated that his requested invitees had arrived. The eight Cardinals, not one in their traditional garb, walked through his office door and quietly moved around the room. A large table had been set up at the far end with nine chairs neatly lined up behind it.

"Good morning, all," the Pope greeted them in low tones.

"Good morning, Your Holiness," was repeated around the room.

In the stillness of the moment they all stood at attention like schoolboys waiting to be scolded.

"Thank you for coming here this morning. I have requested your presence to discuss the matters at hand. I would like to speak to what we have done, all of us. As you all recall, we had voted not to accept the offer from GeneQwest. Mr. Gordon Lynch has departed this Earth and left us as helpless custodians. We can only watch as millions die. Can we sit here now and do nothing? I believe that in the eyes of God we have chosen the wrong path. He has given us free will and our mortal weakness has led us astray. We must retrace our steps, repent and confess."

"I would like to add to your thoughts Your Holiness, if I may?" said Cardinal Joos.

"Certainly," replied the Pope.

"If we reveal what we have done, I believe it will be the end of our Church as we know it. It will crush all faith and belief in God, and leave the faithful spiritually bankrupt."

"And do you believe that this spiritual bankruptcy you talk about will make a difference?" asked the Pope.

"I do. If people lose their belief in our Heavenly Father and life everlasting, they will be stripped of their reason to live a Christian life. It will destroy the foundations of the Church and lead to anarchy. At least we could leave people with hope in their last days. It might comfort them if they knew God was waiting with open arms."

"So it is your understanding that it would be better to say nothing?"

"It is," replied Cardinal Joos.

"I would like to hear from the rest of you," said the Pope, glancing around the table.

"I never thought this day would come. I have always believed in God and I will always do so. I do not know which way is right or which way is wrong, but I see God's hand in everything," said Cardinal Dulles.

"Thank you Cardinal Dulles. I believe your point is well taken and I think that most of us feel the same way. Let me add one final thought. Are we to assume that God has given up on us? After all the sins we have committed against Him and ourselves is He turning His back on us? I can't believe that. He is our loving Savior. Have we committed such sins that we cannot repent, and He cannot forgive us? By what justification are we to continue with this deception?" asked the Pope.

"Your Holiness, can I add a word on this matter?" asked Cardinal Willebrands.

With a nod, the Pope indicated that he had the floor.

"Thank you. I believe we cannot announce what

has happened within our inner circle and this is for two reasons. First, if people knew what our true motivation was, we would lose our ability to lead and advise if we are still here at all after the news breaks. Secondly, we open the door to other faiths of the world to grow in numbers and displace us. Can you imagine what this world would be like if we let Christianity die? Our two-thousand year effort for the souls of the faithful would have been for nothing. We cannot open this Pandora's Box. We must protect the world from itself."

"Your reasoning should never be heard outside this room. We should never be in a contest for souls; God does not work that way," said the Pope. "He wants us to come to Him of our own free will. Is it right that we influence people of other faiths to join us or face the consequences? If we assume that is so, after what has happened recently, I believe we have won that contest.

"Gentlemen, we must halt this deception. I believe that we must follow what we know is right. We have always lived through our faith and right now I believe we are losing touch with the whole meaning behind it. We have lost sight of why we turn to God. He is right in front of us every day in the wonder of life and His gift to us of life everlasting. What we are talking about now is dividing up the souls of people like an army taking prisoners. This must cease. God works through each soul differently. Let us leave it to Him to show us the way.

"My brothers, I have come to a decision on our course of action. Tomorrow evening I will announce the truth to the world. That is my decision. Please be aware that a backlash will probably occur, but we must sacrifice ourselves to help others. It is what Jesus did for us; it is now our turn to repay His love."

Leaving the room, each of the Cardinals dealt with the news, some with relief and some with embarrassment. They staggered out like defeated boxers heading to a recovery room.

Pope John remained behind waiting for the last Cardinal to leave. He closed the double doors and headed for the nearest chair. Limp from worry he slumped down into the brown leather chair. His weathered hands joined together at his belt buckle forming the triangle of prayer. Eyes closed, he prayed in silence, waiting for God's answer.

Chapter 45

July 11th

"Alberto, I will need you to set up a worldwide telecast for this evening. Can you arrange it?"

"I believe I can, but I will have to use our station to broadcast it. There won't be enough time to engage the networks but I am sure they will pick up our feed in a rebroadcast format. I will confirm this, but I am confident that we can use our facilities here."

"Excellent, I will leave the rest to you, just let me know the timing "

"I will, Your Holiness."

"Thank you, Alberto."

In an hour the Pope's phone vibrated in his pocket. "Yes, Alberto?"

"Your Holiness, I wanted to inform you that we are confirmed for tonight at 7pm."

"Thank you for your promptness. I will be ready."

His next call was a direct dial to the President. "Mr. President, this is Pope John speaking. I would like you to know in advance that I will be speaking tonight on television here in Rome. I will be announcing the discovery of an antidote to MG-J12."

"Thank you, Your Holiness, I appreciate you informing me of this. When will this be occurring?"

"I will be announcing it within the next half hour."

"Alright. Have your people send me the details. I'll be listening. And congratulations."

The President placed his phone back on the desk and reached for his remote control.

Pope John slowly pulled a vestment over his head, careful not to crease or stain the white material lest the cameras pick up any imperfections in his attire. His silver and gold cross was prominently displayed and hairpins fastened his skullcap to his head assuring no malfunctions during his delivery. Slipping on his loafer-styled brown shoes he was ready to begin his walk to the Vatican's broadcast building to give his message. Outside his door Alberto waited to assist him through the maze of underground passageways that led to the building.

"I see you are ready, Your Holiness."

"Yes, I am prepared and anxious to spread the good news," smiled the Pope.

"We are all ready for you. Let's proceed shall we?" said Alberto.

Together the two veterans made their way underground until they arrived at the elevator to take them up to the studios of the broadcast building. Outside the old elevator, the crew waited to prepare the Pope for his television appearance.

The red coat of arms formed the backdrop behind a regal high back engraved chair that sat on a bias at the perfect angle to capture the Pope's facial expressions and hand movements on camera.

The Pope began.

"Tonight I am speaking to my brothers and sisters in Christ and to all the people of the world whatever your faith may be. I bring a message of hope.

"After all the pain and suffering that the people of the world have endured over the last year, I would like to share with you some developments that have come to light through the grace of God. Through the efforts of the Vatican Academy of Science, it appears that the Catholic Church has been chosen to lead humanity to salvation. We intend to share our recent revelation with all faiths.

"Our effort to eliminate this plague of destruction has tested us to limits never seen before in history. It has tested our capabilities as human beings, it has tested our love for each other but most of all it has tested our faith: faith in each other, faith in God and faith in the human race. I come to you today to announce that we have worked to find God's healing hand in the midst of this devastation, and we have found it.

"Our researchers at the Academy of Sciences along with a team of scientists from around the world have discovered a cure for MG-J12. Through the grace of God these men and women have battled the enemy and defeated it. God has worked through them to show us the way. To set our mortal salvation in motion requires an antidote, one that we have and that we will share with all. We will work the World Health Organization to distribute this remedy as soon as possible.

"God has tested us; He has asked us to look inside, truly inside ourselves to find Him, to find faith. That faith is within all of us. Through prayer and true belief in God, in whatever form He takes for you and the vaccine which you will shortly receive, a dormant gene is activated to eradicate MG-J12. Today is a great day for humanity: it proves to all of us that God is truly here: He walks among us, He walks beside us. As written in the scriptures, God promised Noah that he would never again destroy all life. He has honoured his promise.

"To all the people of the world we say that this is not the end of mankind, this is the rebirth of a new humanity, a kinder, more loving global community. So believe, pray and seek God's remedy and you will overcome this plague to enjoy the rest of your life until God truly requests your presence by His side. May peace be with you."

Chapter 46

It was noon the next day when the Pope left his chambers. Sunlight shone through the corridor windows, warming the marble walls and the polished floor beneath his slippers. The sealed box containing all the copies of Gordon's proposal rested in his arms. He walked for ten minutes before arriving at his private entrance to the Vatican Secret Archives. The wooden door opened on its hinges with a squeal, exposing well-worn plain stone floors that lead down a long corridor. In the ancient hallway, electric sensors flicked on the lights as he travelled under the grey conduit electrical supply line's path to a security door. He stopped, lowered the box to the floor and ran his hand over the green glow of the fingerprint reader on the wall. The door opened revealing row upon row of bookshelves reaching to the ceiling.

The history of the Christian world was documented in this room. The musky smell of old paper barely permeated the climate-controlled air. The two-storey, bunker-type room was protected and maintained by a small group of archivists, the curators of the past. The Pope headed in direction of Phillip Masse the Archivist. Bowing in anticipation, Phillip watched the Pope's slippers heading toward him.

It was a rare event that the Pope would come to the archives without an assistant; in fact, Phillip had never seen this before. Once in front of Phillip, the Pope motioned for him to raise his head.

"Hello Phillip," said the Pope.

"Hello, Your Holiness. What a privilege it is for me to serve you today. I trust your health is returning?"

"Thank you, yes it is. I will need your help in assisting me with a request."

"Absolutely. I am at your service, Your Holiness. Now, how can I be of assistance?"

"I require that this box is archived but not opened."

"Certainly, Your Holiness, can I ask what it contains?"

"I would prefer that you just enter the date," said the Pope.

"Absolutely, Your Holiness."

Heading off to the computerized catalogue, Phillip proceeded to quickly archive the box according to the Pope's request. Returning minutes later he confirmed it had been entered.

"Thank you, Phillip, one last request."

"However I can be of service," nodded Phillip.

"Please ensure that the box is placed away from easy access."

"I understand. We do have an area where such documents reside; I will make sure it is placed with them. It was an honour to serve you," Phillip answered, bowing at the same time.

Task completed, the Pope headed back to his quarters through his usual route above ground. The outside air was distinctly different - better - and sitting down at his desk, he felt relief for the first time in months.

Phillip headed down an aisle row carrying the box. There were over fifty miles of bookshelves in the library. Using a small stepladder, Phillip positioned the non-descript box high on a shelf among the others and then returned to his work.

Chapter 47

July 11th

Henry sliced open the small envelope that appeared under his door and pulled out a pocket sized invitation card that requesting a meeting with the Pope at 1pm that afternoon. No reply was required; it was understood that he would attend.

"Hello Your Holiness, I hope you are regaining your strength. You requested a meeting?" Cardinal Hickey said as he entered the Pope's office at the appointed hour.

"Thank you, Cardinal Hickey. Yes, I am feeling stronger every day. Please take a chair," he said pointing to the one next to the desk.

"I am glad," said Cardinal Hickey "We can now move forward in helping others in their faith."

"Yes, well that is why I asked to talk to you this morning; I wanted to inform you of our next step."

"Excellent, Your Holiness. I look forward to working together toward our goal."

"Cardinal Hickey…" he paused, looking for the right words. "Henry, I am requesting that you step down and return to civilian life."

"Your Holiness?" Henry heard the Pope's request echoing in his ears. "Your Holiness, I can't understand this."

"Henry, before you continue, I know what you have been plotting behind the scenes. I have it on good authority that your efforts to influence our decision were financially motivated. I have decided that it is best that you step away from the whole situation."

"Ok, let me understand this. Are you asking to step away completely, to resign from the Catholic Church totally, I mean… just disappear?"

"Yes, I am afraid that is correct," Pope John said.

"Why would you ask this of me, when you obviously know others were involved?" Henry asked weakly, feeling the room spinning around him.

"I feel it would be best given the situation."

"Situation? What situation are you referring to?"

"Henry, I know that you accepted money from a certain party and the motivation behind this payment was to influence our decision, to shape the outcome. As you are well aware, financially motivated actions are grounds for excommunication. I have also discovered a large transfer of funds to one of Mr. Lynch's companies. This, combined with your acceptance of his money, leaves me with no choice. I must ask you to step down. You know I have the authority to make this happen. It is up to you how you want this to look and I don't think you would like the alternative, would you?"

"Alternative? You mean excommunication? After all I've done for the Church you expect me to just leave quietly?"

"Yes, Henry, that would be the preferred course. I know it is a little disturbing. Let me just say that we have decided to take a different route from the one that you coordinated."

Cardinal Hickey sat motionless. His legs felt both weak and heavy as lead. He was not sure that he could stand up without falling.

"I guess you leave me no choice. I will pack my belongings and head back to New York. Is there anything I can say that might change this?" he asked, playing for time.

"I am afraid not Henry. It has been decided. We

will handle this with the utmost discretion. I can assure you that you will not be implicated in anything. You have my word on this."

"I still can't believe this is happening," Henry Hickey said as he rose slowly and turned towards the office door. "Goodbye, Your Holiness," he said, a rote courtesy that he would never recall saying.

"Goodbye Henry," said Pope John.

The door closed behind him as he walked down the arched hallway.

Chapter 48

July 12th
Illumina Labs, Bristol

The shop windows reflected the dying sunlight as James closed the door to the lab and headed down Broad Street. He stopped to watch as two cars jousted for position in the narrow street, then he continued on, taking in the aroma of the damp streets, the hanging baskets of flowers and the coffee houses.

When cigarette smoke combined with the smell of stale beer he knew he was close to a pub. From his side of the street he could see the pub patrons hanging outside the door puffing away. Streetlights hummed as they flickered to life, slowly illuminating the cobblestone sidewalks.

He was early for his meeting with Sara so he wandered slowly in the direction of Dickens' Pub, taking in the sights of life on the street. Groups of people were enjoying the start of the evening, passing their limited time with friends, making sure they didn't waste a minute of what was left.

James turned onto a side street, killing time and curious about the incessant cheering that filled the air. He thought it might be keen football fans, cheering when the home side scored a goal, but as he continued down the street he soon realized that there was no football game. People were dancing and hugging each other in celebration. Within spitting distance of the rowdy group, he asked a straggler if it was someone's birthday.

"Are you kidding me mate, haven't you heard?"

"I guess I haven't. What is it that I haven't heard?"

"It's fucking brilliant it is, the Pope guy, he was on the telly just about half an hour ago, he announced that they had found out what all this shit is about. He said they have found the cure for this fucking virus."

"Really, and what was it?"

"I don't really know, to tell you the truth, I had too many pints by then, but my mates tell me that they have figured it out. So we will be sticking around a bit longer I guess mate, they thought we were done for, you know what I mean?"

"Sort of I guess. Thanks for the information."

"Yeah, no worries mate, come on in and let me buy you a pint, come on."

"Ah, thanks anyway, I'm meeting someone just up the road from here," James said, pulling away from his new friend.

"Whatever you say mate. Cheers!" he said hoisting his half-finished pint of lager in the air like a trophy from a recent win.

James backtracked to Broad Street, quickening his pace. He didn't want to be late meeting Sara again. Within sight of the glowing lights of the pub again, he watched as the celebratory scene was repeated at every establishment that was serving beer and every restaurant and shop.

Pulling the oversized brass handle of the pub's door, he was immediately met with a wall of cheers and singing. Looking around for Sara, he saw her cloud of blonde hair. She was sitting at a corner table trying to stay clear of the rowdy crowds.

"So, you picked a nice quiet place," joked James as he stood at her table.

"Oh, hi James," she beamed up at him. "Well it was a nice quiet place until the announcement."

"Yes, I heard about it on the way over here. What

the hell did he say?"

"Well, let's see, he basically said their Academy had found the secret to our survival."

"Wow, that's quite the claim."

"I know, but they say that they have proof, and that they have tested it. All their top geneticists and microbiologists confirm that it works."

"So, is it a pill, or serum, or what? Have they bottled the elixir?" He asked.

"Something like that. There is an antidote, and I'm not sure what form it will be in."

"Anything else?" James asked.

"No, should there be?"

"No, I was just wondering if there were more details."

"I am just telling you what I heard."

"Amazing, truly amazing. Well if it works, we should start taking it right now," James said sarcastically.

"James, come on. I think you know it will work, don't you? The Vatican is putting their slant on it but saying that it was God who gave them the answer, but both you and I know that's not exactly correct, don't we?"

"Well maybe it did come from a higher power? Maybe He didn't rest on the seventh day after all? I think

I remember it being a Sunday when I noticed it," James said smiling. "We both know that science has discovered the solution, Sara. Did God point us in the right direction or was it proven research that gave us the solution? Did we have to lose hundreds of thousands of people for God to make a point? That's too many useless experiments."

"Ever think maybe - just maybe - there isn't always a scientific solution to everything? For some reason humans have always believed in something. Ever ask yourself why?" Sara asked.

"No, I haven't."

"Well, I have," Sara replied. "Question, James: how did your research get in the hands of the Vatican? You couldn't announce it because of Gordon's, shall we say, passing, and you were the only one with the tissue that led you to find out about it. So how did the Vatican figure it out?"

"Not sure. Must have been divine intervention." James smiled.

Chapter 49

July 21st

Returning home after meeting with James at the pub, Sara knew the information about James would impact her plans. Settling into her brown leather chair facing the window she picked up the phone and punched the numbers she had hit many times. After two rings the familiar voice thundered at the other end.

"Hello?"

"Hi Dad, why are you shouting?"

"Sorry dear, am I? Must be my hearing, getting old you know."

"Right. Well it seems that things have fallen into place without much effort on our part. I have been sending you updates on the goings on. Have you been getting them?"

"Yes, sweetie thanks, very interesting."

"Dad, there is another piece of information that I have found out that will aid our efforts."

"Great, and what might that be?"

"It turns out I didn't have to gather the information from Illumina. The intelligence will be coming in one package: James Mitchell."

"Sorry Sara, you lost me there, what do you mean by James Mitchell?"

"James Mitchell killed Gordon."

A loud "WHAT?!" broke the silence on the other end.

"Yep, James confessed to me the other night. He did it by slowly increasing a poison in Gordon's medication."

"That is unbelievable. Quiet, reserved, educated James turns out to be a murderer. I just can't get that through my head."

"So Dad, this leaves some options open to us. We can now include him in our plans and he could never refuse. We have the information that will keep him with us for as long as it takes."

"My daughter, the schemer," John Abbott smiled through the phone.

"I had a good teacher."

"That you did, my dear, that you did. So where do we go from here?"

"I thought we could propose our plan to James. With him onboard we can take GeneQwest to new heights. Being the majority shareholder we will be able to negotiate from a position of strength."

"Sounds good to me."

"Ok, I'll keep you in the loop. Bye, Dad."

"Bye Sara, I'll wait to hear from you. Hey, did he ever make the connection?"

"No, but I did tell him I was married and that it didn't last very long. He never had a clue that I was your daughter."

Chapter 50

July 23rd

Costa Coffee on the corner of Queen's Avenue and Elmdale was three blocks from Illumina and a thirty-minute walk from James's flat. Eyeing his watch, James monitored his pace to arrive for his meeting with John Abbott. He pulled the oversized door open at exactly 8pm, walked in and surveyed the coffee shop for the American.

Waiting by the counter, James pretended to be interested in the various pictures of coffee-inspired art. Suddenly he felt a large hand rest on his right shoulder, and he turned to stare at the person behind him.

"Hi. You must be James," a deep voice said.

"Yes I am," James said, shaking John's extended hand.

"John Abbott. It is a pleasure to finally meet you."

"Shall we grab a table?"

"Yes," said James.

Leading the way, James mindlessly followed the large framed man. He had recognized him; he had seen him before. It couldn't be the same person, could it? John Abbott was the man in the picture frame in Sara's office. Why would she have a picture of him? Who was he to her?

"So, here we are, James. I have heard lots about you lately, you know. Some good, some not so good."

James only heard every other word. He was retrieving information from his memory, trying to connect the dots while listening to a jumble of words.

"Sorry, I didn't catch that." He wrestled to get out some recognizable words.

"I was saying that I have heard good things about you and some not so good things."

"I guess that could be true about all of us," James said nervously.

"We all have skeletons in the closet, it just depends if they are still talking," John chuckled. "How long have you been working for Illumina?"

"This will be my sixth year."

"Been good to you, James?"

"Yes, very good, some ups and downs like any place."

"Good to hear. That is what I want to continue with. Good people, interesting work and great achievements, agreed?"

"Yes, certainly."

"So with that said, let's talk."

"Ok, about what?"

"The future."

"Right."

"So remember I mentioned to you, some good and some bad?"

"Yes."

"Well, I know that you worked very closely with Gordon."

"Yes, that's right."

"I have been reviewing some of the reports that you submitted to the board. In reading them a certain action came to my attention that related to our recently departed Mr. Lynch."

James sensed his body shift into defense mode and his hands began to get clammy. His mouth was dry and he could feel his heart racing. He tried to keep his hand steady as he sipped his coffee.

"I'm not sure what you mean. Mr. Lynch and I had a good business relationship."

"I am sure you did. He dictated and you followed."

"Not quite like that but sometimes."

"James," John said, pushing his coffee cup forward to make his point, "I have an offer that might be of interest to you. In fact I believe that it will be so interesting to you that you won't say no."

"I am kind of a free agent now, to use an American term."

"I guess you are, but hear me out and then we can talk. I have it from a very reliable source that you were involved in some... let's say... 'dubious actions' in regards to Mr. Lynch's death. Would I be right about that?"

Again James could feel his heartbeat increase, pushing blood to his face. He could feel his cheeks turning red.

"I am not sure what you mean. I can assure you Mr. Lynch died of natural causes. I am sure that his death certificate corroborates that."

"Maybe it does, but I know otherwise, and so do you."

"Well you can think what you want."

"Fair enough, but before we go any further with this cat and mouse charade, let me tell you who I am. I'm Sara's father."

All blood that was in James face had vanished in a moment. Suddenly pale and motionless, James stared at John's face, looking right through to the wall behind.

"Did you hear me James?"

James froze, hearing the words but unable to reply.

"James, James…."

Eyes widened and refocused on John's slightly pitted skin.

"I did hear you. So?"

"Sara told me everything, just as you told her. But let's not point fingers or worry about the past, let's focus on the future: our future."

"Our future?"

"Yes, our future James," John said, smiling.

"Do we have a future?"

"Sure we do."

"So if you think you know what I did, you must think you know why I did it."

"James, James, I am not here to pass judgment. I

am here to make you a proposition."

"A proposition?" queried James.

"Here it is in a nutshell: stay with Illumina and I - we - will do good things and make some money along the way."

James paused to consider this before he spoke.

"I don't really care about money John. As you said, let's forget about the past."

"Unfortunately for you, James, I know I said that, but what I meant was that I will let you forget your past. I will remember it."

"Leaving me where?" asked James.

"Leaving you in a position we would describe in the States as between a rock and a hard place."

Bringing the coffee cup to his dry lips, James swallowed the last of the lukewarm liquid. "What exactly are you offering?"

"For you to stay on at Illumina, to work in research and development for the greater good of society."

"Mr. Abbott, I have heard that line before. Gordon fed me the same rhetoric when really he had other motivations. What are yours?"

"I'll cut to the chase: you don't have much choice,

you either stay with Illumina or I go to the authorities. You can lead teams of whomever you want but I want copyright on whatever you discover. I want to own your research so everyone will have to come to us to develop anything pertaining to it. We will be the owners of the future."

"And how does fit in with doing good things?"

"I will finance global health. All I want is some remuneration for that risk; I don't think that is too much to ask. In effect, I want to patent the genetic material that will benefit the masses. I'd like you to map genetic material that will address disease, the medically important genes."

"We would be patenting nature in the interest of profit. How is that a good thing?" James repeated.

"We will work on the sequencing for diabetes first, and then work towards curing cancer. Are you in?"

Pushing his chair back James locked his hands behind his head, running the scenarios around in his mind. He looked back at John. "And what if I say no?"

"Well, there might be times sitting in that cell that you may have wished you hadn't."

The white noise of the coffee shop was the only sound as the men stared at each other.

James stood up. "I believe we have an understanding. Let's leave it at that."

"Great to have you on board." John smiled up at James.

Chapter 51

Sitting on his sofa in New York, Henry Hickey played with the ears of the young beagle sitting by his side. Together they watched the unfolding of the day's events. A recovered Pope was paraded around Rome verifying his health. Streets were overflowing with people coming to get a glimpse of the revitalized Pope. Cameras followed the Popemobile through the streets where people hanging out of office windows waved the Vatican flag, cheering as he went by. More than a celebration, it was a return to normalcy for millions of viewers.

Henry moved closer to his black cordless phone, picked it up and started to dial, then laid it back in its holder. He rubbed his hand over his forehead as he watched the proceedings. Total adulation for His Holiness was evident around every corner and on every street.

Henry reached for the phone again, more confidently this time, and punched zero.

"Hello, can I help you?"

"Yes, can you give me the number of the New York Times?" asked Henry. "Thank you."

He dialed the digits, waited for the voice at the other end.

"Good morning, New York Times, how can I direct your call?

"Morning, can you put me through to Peter Turner please?"

"Just one moment sir and I will connect you."

"Hello, Pete Turner here."

"Hello Mr. Turner, my name is Henry Hickey. Is it possible that we can meet today? I have a story you might be interested in."

Epilogue

New Mexico, U.S.A.

At noon, just off a dusty side road, a beige trailer stood with its siding pockmarked by pellets of sand. Matt and Gillian could see their home away from home from their new dig. Their worn paint brushes that had brushed away millenniums of earth were resting on a nearby boulder.

Gillian called Matt over to a new part of the dig where she had uncovered an interesting find.

"Matt, see that, what the hell do you think that is?"

"I can't tell from here. Need to get it out of the ground first, then we both can take a better look."

Within a few hours they had carefully removed all the sand and debris from around the sample.

"Careful, I'm not sure what the hell it is. I have never seen anything like that before," said Matt.

"I can attest to that. It sure looks weird, any ideas at all?'

"Nope, and you know what happened last time we found something like this."

"Yes I do, you don't have to remind me again," said Gillian. "What do we do with it?" she said.

"Let's just put it in the truck and let someone else have a look at it. Are you good with that?"

"For sure," said Gillian. "For sure."

Made in the USA
Charleston, SC
28 November 2012